Her cart jolted. She looked and saw she'd bumped into someone. Someone wearing tennis shoes. Which probably meant the back of his ankles would really hurt. "I'm so sorry."

The man lifted his right foot a bit as he turned to face her. "No prob— You?"

It couldn't be. It simply was not possible. There stood the same man she'd run into at the barn and on the sidewalk. She was normally a very careful person, but it seemed as if some weird force propelled her to wound this man in some way.

Her cheeks warmed and her hands shook slightly until she gripped the cart handle. "I—I don't know what to say."

A smile bowed the man's lips, and Johanna couldn't help but admit how cute he was. He extended his hand. "I think I'd better introduce myself to you before you need to notify my family."

Johanna frowned. "Notify your family?"

"Yeah. The next time you run into me you may put me in the hospital."

JENNIFER JOHNSON and her unbelievably supportive husband, Albert, are happily married and raising Brooke, Hayley, and Allie, the three cutest young ladies on the planet. Besides being a middle school teacher, Jennifer loves to read, write, and chauffeur her girls. She is a member of American Christian Fiction Writers. Blessed beyond measure, Jennifer hopes to always think like a child—bigger than imaginable and with complete faith. Send her a note at jenwrites4god@bellsouth.net.

Books by Jennifer Johnson

HEARTSONG PRESENTS

Don't miss out on any of our super romances. Write to us at the following address for information on our newest releases and club information.

Heartsong Presents Readers' Service
PO Box 721
Uhrichsville, OH 44683

Or visit www.heartsongpresents.com

Game
of Love

Jennifer Johnson

Heartsong Presents

To my dear friend and critique partner, Rose McCauley. I met this wonderful woman at the first national ACRW (now ACFW) writing conference. Since then she has been one of my greatest encouragers. From laughing off my scatterbrained ways when I forget clothes for conference, to inviting everyone who enters the store where I'm signing to buy one of my books, to editing two to four chapters a day for a week (which she did for this story), Rose has been a constant smile in my life. Thank you, Rose. I love you.

A note from the Author:
I love to hear from my readers! You may correspond with me by writing:

Jennifer Johnson
Author Relations
PO Box 721
Uhrichsville, OH 44683

ISBN 978-1-61626-369-0

GAME OF LOVE

Scripture taken from the Holy Bible, New International Version®. niv®. Copyright © 1973, 1978, 1984 by International Bible Society. Used by permission of Zondervan. All rights reserved.

Our mission is to publish and distribute inspirational products offering exceptional value and biblical encouragement to the masses.

PRINTED IN THE U.S.A.

one

Johanna Smith took a step away from the wedding cake table and wiped her brow with the back of her hand. She admired the three-tiered, buttercream fondant-covered creation her mother had designed. Light-yellow and light-pink roses overlapped each other and covered the top of the cake. White fondant that her mother had made to look like ribbons circled the bottom of each tier with a small bouquet of yellow and pink roses resting on the left side of the middle tier and on the right side of the bottom tier. "Mama, this is the prettiest one yet."

A full smile framed her mother's lips. "Thanks, Johanna." She wiped her hands on the front of her dark-blue denim skirt then pointed at the cake. "I had such a time with the flowers on the middle tier. I was afraid they'd never look right."

Johanna stepped closer to the cake, inspecting the part her mother mentioned. Her mother had to add an extra few roses to that bouquet to get it to sit properly, but her mother had a natural touch when it came to decorating pastry, and the cake looked exquisite. "If it tastes as good as it looks, they're in for a real treat."

"Made-from-scratch French vanilla on the top and bottom tiers and dark chocolate on the middle one—it better be good."

Johanna chuckled softly. "Mama, your cakes are always delicious." She peered around the barn-turned-reception-area. Normally, one of her younger sisters would have helped their mother deliver the wedding cake, as Johanna veered away from crowds. But she'd been so intrigued by the idea of holding a reception in a barn that she'd wanted to see how it looked.

Her gaze drank in the perfectly arranged bales of hay along three walls of the barn. Bouquets of pink and yellow roses, baby's breath, and daisies had been tucked into the hay bales in various places. Yellow and pink iridescent balloons hung from the rafters above the bales. The barn doors stood open and the white satin sashes wrapped along the top and sides of the opening created a second wedding arch. Large light-yellow bows and pink roses were tied every few feet all the way around.

Several circular tables, twenty or more if Johanna guessed correctly, rested along the center of the barn floor. Some of them were already decorated with the smallest hay bales she'd ever seen, probably only one foot long, that held smaller versions of the same bouquets gracing the bales lining the walls.

She looked at her mother, who also drank in the elaborate decorations. "This has got to be the most beautiful barn I've ever seen."

"It smells wonderful, too."

Johanna sucked in a deep breath. The scent of roses mingled with hay hovered in the air, but the soft scent of the horses that lived in the barn still lingered. The mixture brought a smile to her lips. "It's perfect, isn't it?"

"It is, but we'd best stop dawdling."

Johanna turned back toward her mother, who began to work feverishly gathering the supplies. After scooping up her mother's touch-up instruments and a few small plastic bags, she sneaked one last peek at the open room. Not usually one to fret over froufrou things, Johanna couldn't stop the niggling of desire to be planning her own wedding.

She was young in the world's eyes. She knew that. But she and her family had never lived by the world's standards. Her father, a conservative minister of a small country church in Hickory Hill, had raised her to love the Lord above all else. She'd been taught how to be a lady and how to take care of a home while learning all of her pre-college schooling at her mother's hip. And she'd witnessed a love between her parents that she'd longed for since her early adolescence.

Besides, she felt much older than her peers. Though she'd stayed in her parents' home, she'd graduated from a nearby college with a degree in English. She enjoyed her job at the public library in the nearby town of River Run. But her heart longed for a husband and children to care for. *Maybe the children could wait a few years. I am only twenty-one. But still, I'd love for God to reveal His husband for me.*

Knowing her mother would be unhappy with her meandering, Johanna turned on her heels and stepped forward. She slammed into something solid. The man looked as surprised as Johanna when her mother's touch-up materials fell to the ground, as did a cardboard box of small plastic bottles of bubbles. On impact, several of the bottles popped out of the box and spilled all over the floor. Johanna gasped at the unexpected collision and placed her hand on her chest as she stepped backward. Her heel didn't quite reach the floor as she smashed a bottle of bubbles, sending the soapy substance squirting out of the side. She lost her footing and started to fall backward when the man in front of her reached forward and grabbed hold of her then smashed her into his chest.

Heat rushed up her neck and wrapped around her cheeks as she gathered her balance then pushed away from him. She found it hard to speak past her embarrassment as she peered up then away from the very handsome, all-dressed-up-in-a-tuxedo fellow. "I am so sorry." She bent down and started to pick up the bottles and toss them in the cardboard box that had landed to her right.

A frustrated sigh seeped from the man's lips, making her feel even worse. "It's okay," he mumbled.

She leaned forward to reach a stray bottle, grabbed it, then flipped her head back to look up at him to apologize once more. The top of her head connected with him. Hard. A slight squeal slipped from her lips and a moan fell from his. She touched the top of her head and looked up at the guy. Blood trickled down his bottom lip.

"Oh my. I'm so sorry." She reached in the front pockets of her capris, praying she had a tissue of some kind in one of them. She—didn't. She looked around the room. The only tissues or napkins she spied were already part of the table decorations. She looked back at the man. He hadn't moved, just stood sucking blood from his bottom lip and staring at her as if she'd lost her mind.

Tears welled in her eyes and she tried to bite them back. She loathed her typical, horrible nervous response to any situation that had her flustered. Painfully shy—and having lived most of her life sheltered in what she deemed the best of ways—she'd never fully learned how to handle an embarrassing situation such as this.

The expression of complete reproof and disdain tracing the man's face shook her already melting countenance. Growing more mortified by the second, she noted a dot of crimson blood on the front of his white shirt. Before the tears could stream down her face, she scooped up her mother's materials and raced out the door, leaving the man with the bulk of the mess to clean up.

I should go back. I shouldn't just leave the mess to that man. God, I'm just so embarrassed. I'm never that clumsy.

She reached the van. She simply couldn't go back now. Thankful her mother still arranged things in the back, Johanna slipped into the passenger's seat. She pulled down the visor and peered at her reflection. Her cheeks were flushed and her eyes red and puffy. She blinked several times and gently patted her cheeks. After loosening her ponytail, she pulled down a few long blond strands around her temples to help disguise her eyes. She did not want to have to explain her emotions to her mother.

Her mother's voice sounded from the back of the van. "It looked as if they're going to have a beautiful reception."

"Yes." Johanna tried to sound emotionless as she sucked in a few more breaths. The expression of contempt in the man's perfect blend of green and blue eyes still seemed to float around in her mind, and she inwardly chastised herself that she continued to feel waves of embarrassment.

"I don't really know the family, but they seem like

wonderful Christians. You'd think we'd know more people from River Run. After all, we only live ten miles from here." A loud snap sounded from the rear of the van, and Johanna knew her mother had put the backseat in place.

"Mm-hmm." Johanna lifted the visor and patted her cheeks one last time. She was a grown woman. Rationally, she knew she shouldn't get so upset. She sat up straight and braced herself for her mother to get in the driver's seat. Praying her face looked normal, she sucked in her breath when her mom slipped inside.

She could feel her mother's gaze upon her for what seemed like an eternity. Finally turning to face her mother, she said, "Mama, I—"

Her mother patted her leg. "Johanna, I know you long for a husband and a home of your own. The time is coming. I'm not sure why Gavin drags his feet, but—"

Johanna looked out the window beside her seat. Her mother misunderstood her emotions. At that moment, she was not longing for her future life. And she hoped Gavin dragged his feet until, well, until forever. His mother and her mother had always presumed the two would make a match one day, but she didn't have the slightest interest in Gavin Mitchell. And she felt certain he would agree with her sentiments. At least she hoped he would.

She found nothing wrong with the guy. Born one month before her, she and Gavin had spent their entire lives together, from playpen to school lessons to Sunday outings. He was a good Christian man and a true friend. But that was all.

She continued to stare out the window as her mother began to talk about all they needed to do when they got home. Johanna couldn't listen. All she could think about was a pair of blue-green eyes filled with contempt. Though she tried to squelch the feeling, she wondered what they'd look like if the man smiled.

≈

The day just couldn't get any worse for Mike McCauley. It should have been a day of celebration. The last of his friends tying the knot with the woman of his dreams. Which meant that not only should he be happy for his lifelong buddy, he should also be celebrating the fact that for once in their friendship, he'd beaten his three best friends in a bet. A feat he had never accomplished before.

The whole thing had started innocent enough. Seven years ago Mike and his friends, Wyatt, Nick, and Drew, watched as another friend tied the knot. Still young and foolish, the four of them made a bet that whoever was the last of them to get hitched won, and the losers had to help plan and pay for the winner's wedding.

Wyatt had been the first to fall, marrying his high school friend, Gracie. Then Nick married Drew's sister, Addy. And now, Drew, the man who won nearly every bet the four made, decided to lose the bet and marry Nick's cousin, Melody.

Mike was the winner, and yet he was the biggest loser of all.

He looked at his reflection in the bathroom mirror. After that woman practically body slammed him in the barn, he'd had to run over to the main house to try to get the blood out of his shirt. He didn't have to go too far, only 150 yards or so to the main house. In fact, they were using the house to keep the food warm as well as a restroom facility, as needed, but he still didn't have time to be running to unnecessary places. He had to be at the church in thirty minutes.

Growling at his reflection, he'd succeeded in making a quarter-size red stain out of what had been a tiny drop of blood on the white shirt. Not to mention that his bottom lip was slightly swollen around the teeth marks where he'd bitten down hard when his mouth collided with the woman's head.

He'd never seen the blond-haired woman before. He hoped never to see her again. At least not today. He had enough to deal with today.

Even though it had been nine months since his brother drowned, it would still be the first time he'd seen a lot of these friends and family in a group setting. He'd been praying for strength for weeks, especially since he would be bombarded with condolences, comments, and promises of continued prayers. His parents would be attending the ceremony, but not the reception. His mother still carried a lot of bitterness and anger in her heart regarding God's sovereignty. She hadn't been to church or rejoined any of her usual activities since Joe's death. She simply stayed home, only visiting briefly with those who hadn't given up on visiting with her on her good days.

Trying one last time, he pumped a dab of liquid soap onto a paper towel then tried to blot it against the red spot. It simply would not come all the way out, and it was located in a place he could not hide it. With a deep sigh, he threw the paper towels in the trash then walked out of the bathroom.

He gulped when he saw Lacy McRoberts standing in the kitchen doorway. She caught his eye and smiled. He lifted his hand in a hesitant wave, and she made her way toward him. Mike willed himself to remain calm as his heart beat fast and hard against his chest. A cold sweat washed over him and he shifted his weight to be sure his extremities still worked.

He'd had a crush on Lacy for years. Three, to be exact. At first, he'd just been too bashful to admit his feelings for her. Then, he'd decided not to pursue her because he thought he might be able to win the bet. Then, he found himself longing for what he saw happening between Nick and Addy and he almost asked her out two years ago, but Drew picked at him a bit, and Mike grew determined to wait a bit longer. After all, he had to beat Drew at something.

Then, Drew fell for Melody and Mike determined to ask Lacy on a date. But his brother died in the accident and all he could think about was his grief and holding on to God and caring for his parents. *But, Lord, today is the day. I promised You that today I'd ask her. It's time to move forward.*

"Here she comes. You gonna ask her out?"

Mike jumped at the sound of Nick's voice behind him. He turned and saw his friend wink as he carried a small circular table out the back door. With friends as exhausting as his, it was no wonder Mike hadn't asked the woman out. At the end of the day, he was just flat-out too tired.

"Hi, Mike."

Mike turned again and Lacy already stood in front of him. He wondered if she'd heard what Nick said. He couldn't imagine that she missed it. It wasn't as if Nick's deep voice didn't already boom through a room even when he whispered. Mike cleared his throat. "Hi, Lacy." He nodded toward her purple dress. "You look pretty."

"Thanks. So do you." Mike sucked in his breath when her gaze took in the length of him. She frowned as she pointed to the bloodstain. "What happened?"

He touched his finger to his mouth. "Bit my lip."

"Oh no."

Mike stiffened when she reached up and touched his lip. He'd never known her to be forward in any way, but then he'd never really known her outside of the diner, either. Not since they were kids, anyway.

She rummaged through the small silver bag that hung from her shoulder. "I always keep a stain remover pen with me."

She pulled out the orange device and pulled off the top. Mike felt his cheeks warm when she flattened his shirt against his chest with her left hand then dabbed the pen against the spot with her right.

She stepped back and put the lid back on the pen then smiled up at him. "All gone."

He prayed his neck and cheeks weren't as red as he feared as he looked down at the spot. Sure enough, she'd gotten the stain out. He looked back at her and smiled. "That is terrific. Thanks so much." He laughed. "I was afraid I was going to be in big trouble."

Lacy giggled then twisted her lips into a pout as she touched his bottom lip again. "I wish I could do something to help you with that."

He'd never known the woman to be so bold, and yet he'd never felt so attracted to her. He liked the perkiness in her personality, something he'd never seen at the diner. Before he'd only been attracted to her looks, but maybe she was a woman who would keep him on his toes as well.

The shyness he'd always known tried to creep its way up his spine. He could feel himself starting to back away. *God, help me move forward. Open my mouth.*

He cleared his throat. "Lacy, would you like to go to dinner with me this week?"

Squinting at him, Lacy bit her bottom lip. She crossed her arms in front of her chest and studied him for what seemed like hours. Finally, her mouth broke into a smile and she nodded. "Mike McCauley, I seriously thought you'd never ask."

two

Johanna grabbed her Bible and journal off the nightstand and shoved them into her tote bag with the embroidered bookworm on the front. She pulled a sweater off the hanger and put it on. Though often warm in Kentucky in May, the early hours were still quite cool. As she did every morning, she planned to greet her Savior early in the day with the rising sun.

She walked quietly down the hall. The family's golden retriever hopped up off his bed in her parents' room and joined her. She and Max were the only two members of the family who enjoyed early rising. With the wafting aroma of the coffee she'd preset to brew, she pulled her mug out of the dishwasher, added a spoonful of sugar, a bit of milk, and then the warm, delicious-smelling java. She looked down at Max. "Ya ready?"

Max wagged his tail and walked in a circle, whimpering. Johanna opened the back door. The cool, damp air kissed her face and she zipped up her sweater then slid her feet into her old loafers. She hefted her bag up on her shoulder and pressed the fingers of her right hand against the mug for additional warmth as she shut the door behind her and Max.

In a matter of moments, the sun would rise. She quickened her pace as she walked toward the pond at the top of a slight hill behind their house. Reaching the top, she placed her bag on the bench her father had made several years ago for her to use in this favorite spot. She pulled a hand towel from the bag and spread it out on the bench to avoid getting wet from the morning dew. She sat and watched the horizon.

As if God had been waiting just for her, an orange haze peeked up from the hills to the east. A bright-yellow mound rose from beneath it, giving way to the top of the yellow-white mass of the sun. The plush green springtime grass and lush trees seemed to stand taller, more confidently, as light and warmth bathed them.

"Dear Jesus, Your creation is amazing."

Welcoming her day with the sunrise and a prayer to her Lord had been a ritual since she turned thirteen years old, and she never grew tired of the wonder and majesty of His glory. She opened her journal and wrote her first of the morning's praises, as well as concerns. One concern that weighed heavy on her heart was her sister Amber's desire to attend public school this fall for her senior year.

Johanna had loved being taught by her mother and father, but she was also content with the simpler things, including solitude and inner reflection. Her youngest sister, twelve-year-old Bethany, was a lot like Johanna. Amber, on the other hand, was boisterous and social. She exhibited a special giftedness in music, and at almost seventeen, longed to share her talent in a public setting with the hope of gaining a scholarship of some kind.

Johanna finished her scripture reading and writing and looked up at the still pond waters before her. Her mind drifted to the blue-green eyes of the man she'd bumped into. She touched the spot on her head where they'd collided. It still ached, and she wondered if his bottom lip had swollen and to what degree. Had he been able to get the blood spot out of the white shirt? Wearing a tuxedo, he must have been a member of the wedding party. For all she knew, he was the groom.

She cringed at the thought of having busted the groom's mouth on his wedding day. *Lord, I pray he wasn't the groom.*

She'd seen the man for only a brief few moments, but she felt sure she would spot him in an instant. Her mind continually replayed his strong, freshly shaven jaw and chin, his straight nose, and full dark eyebrows, just a shade darker than his sandy-brown hair. But it was his piercing blue-green eyes that haunted her.

She brushed the thought away as she gathered her journal and Bible and shoved them back in her bag. She made her way down the hill and back to the house. Almost an hour had passed. Her family was sure to be up by now. Amber was probably already practicing on the piano while Bethany got her shower. Daddy was most assuredly sitting at the kitchen table talking with Mama while she finished the biscuits and gravy.

It was Tuesday, her day off, and she knew her mother would want her to help fix the birthday cake orders that had to be finished by Wednesday night. Johanna wasn't as good at the decorating, but she could do the baking just fine.

She opened the back door and startled at the sight of Gavin sitting at the kitchen table eating breakfast with her daddy. Her mother looked at her and smiled. If Johanna didn't know the woman better, she'd have thought the look was of pure mischief. Mama placed her hand on Gavin's back. "Hurry up and get ready. Gavin's come to get you.

Remember you promised Sandy you'd help her with spring cleaning today?"

She plopped her tote bag onto the table. "I'd forgotten." She nudged Gavin's shoulder, as he was still her friend despite their parents' matchmaking attempts. "You get here early enough?"

Gavin wiped his mouth with a napkin and swallowed down a large bite. "I don't deny it. I knew if I got here early enough your mama would feed me."

Mama clucked her tongue. "With your mother's last boy as young as he is, I bet she's hardly able to keep up with the laundry. You tell her Johanna will help out any time she needs her."

"Of course I will." Johanna squinted at her mother. She had no qualms with helping Sandy, but she wanted her mother to stop trying to set her up with her friend. She looked back at Gavin. "Just give me a minute to change."

"Don't I get a 'good morning'?" Her daddy stood to his feet and opened his arms. He towered over most men in height and girth, and Johanna always felt loved and protected when he was near.

"Absolutely." She wrapped her arms around the overgrown teddy bear of a man then lifted her face and planted a slight kiss to his jaw. "Have a good day, Daddy."

He patted her back and released her then she raced up the stairs to change clothes and freshen up. She'd completely forgotten about her promise to help Sandy. There'd be little rest to be had at the Mitchell home. With Gavin being the oldest of seven brothers and the youngest still breastfeeding, Johanna could only imagine all Sandy would need her to do.

She pulled her hair up in a quick ponytail and stared at her reflection in the mirror. "Give me strength today, Lord Jesus."

With Bethany finally out of the bathroom, Johanna wiggled her way in and quickly brushed her teeth and washed her face before Amber could complain about needing a shower. Feeling refreshed, she made her way downstairs and grabbed a granola bar from the pantry.

She walked into the kitchen and spied Gavin helping her mother put the dishes in the dishwasher. He would make a good husband one day, but she just didn't feel romantic about Gavin. And though she'd been raised knowing marriage was every bit as much about commitment and friendship as it was love, she still wanted the love. The eros love described in the Bible. A love like Solomon and the Shulamite woman.

Her cheeks warmed and she pushed the thought away. She cleared her throat. "I'm ready, Gavin."

He turned and grinned at her. "Pretty as always."

Mama's knowing yet mischievous smile returned, and Johanna wanted to scold her own mother.

"We'll be leaving now, Mama." Without waiting for her reply, Johanna walked out the back door and toward Gavin's work truck. She hopped inside the passenger's seat and buckled the belt.

Gavin slid in beside her and started it up. "Matchmaking again, huh?"

"As always."

Gavin's deep, guttural laugh sounded through the cab. "They'll never give up."

"I know it. Your mom's going to do the same thing while I'm at your house."

"Yep."

She drank in the rolling hills around her. Gavin lived deeper in the country than she did, and it was nothing surprising to see all kinds of wildlife—raccoons, squirrels, rabbits, and deer. The coyotes she wanted to stay away from, but she knew they mainly showed their faces at night.

Gavin's voice filled the cab again. "I don't know what they're thinking. You and me are just friends."

Johanna shrugged without looking at him. "Always have been."

"Yep. Just friends."

Something in the tone of his voice or in the way he said it didn't seem to sound quite right. She looked at her friend, the guy she'd shared a playpen with. He was her friend. Just her friend. So, why did he all of a sudden look so serious?

ð

Mike had never felt so nervous. He still had a few days to stew over his date with Lacy. Now, he wished he'd just asked her out the day after the wedding. He hadn't planned anything fancy, just a sit-down dinner. He thought he'd drive her into Lexington, where she'd have a bigger selection of restaurants to choose from. But he couldn't focus on his work for fretting over a silly dinner.

Knowing he needed a few things from the hardware store anyway, Mike decided to head into town. Hopefully, he'd be able to talk with Wyatt a bit. Maybe his friend could give him some advice to quell his nerves.

He hadn't told his parents about the date. Since his brother's death, his mother had become overly worried about him and his father. She'd even been to the hospital a few times with severe panic attacks. Though he saw his folks every day at the farm he and his father shared, he tried not to overwhelm them with any of his own concerns, including his first date.

Finally arriving at the hardware store, he walked inside to the sound of a bell over his head. He nodded to his friend who stood behind the counter. "How you doing?"

"Awful." A whiny, female voice sounded in Wyatt's place.

Mike looked against the wall behind the counter and saw Gracie sitting in a chair with a laptop propped on her bulging stomach. Though he'd never tell her, he couldn't imagine how the small woman's belly could get so big. She looked as if she carried a couple of basketballs under that shirt, and both of them fully inflated. Her face seemed all splotchy and even her nose seemed a little wider and flatter, which really weirded him out.

"Honey, you're doing great." Wyatt bent down and kissed the top of his wife's head. "It'll be any day now."

Gracie stuck out her lower lip farther than Mike believed possible. "No, it won't. Melody put a curse on me. She and Drew won't be home for another week, and I won't be having this baby until then." She pushed on the top of her belly while lifting her shoulders and trying to take a breath. "And, I can hardly breathe."

Mike didn't know what to say. She did look rather uncomfortable. Even more so than she had a few days before at the wedding. He knew Melody had told Gracie she'd prayed the Lord wouldn't let her deliver until they returned from the honeymoon. But he was pretty sure that didn't equate to Melody putting a curse on her. He tried to think of something positive. "Where's little Wyatt?"

Big tears pooled in Gracie's eyes then streamed down her cheeks. "I'm so fat I can't even take care of my own son."

"Now Gracie." Wyatt kneeled beside her and rubbed her arm. "You know that's not true. Mom is keeping him while you work on the shop's books. And I told you I'd do them this week."

She sat up, wiped her eyes, and scowled at Wyatt. "Are you saying I can't do my job? I always take care of the books."

"No, honey. I'm saying you need a break. Why don't you take a break?"

The tears returned. "I know I'm an emotional wreck." She looked at Mike. "I'm sorry. Let Wyatt help you with whatever you need."

Wyatt looked at Mike. Obvious by his strained expression, he needed to be needed, and not by Gracie. "What can I help you with?"

"Well, I—"

Wyatt walked around the corner and grabbed Mike by the arm, guiding him toward the plumbing supplies, which just happened to be in the back of the store. "Tell me I love my wife."

"Wyatt, you love your wife."

"Of course, I love my wife, but the last few weeks of pregnancy are absolutely exhausting. Nothing tastes good, and yet she craves everything. Her stomach hurts, her back hurts, her feet hurt. You know what else? My head hurts."

Mike had to bite back a laugh at Wyatt's serious yet frustrated expression.

Wyatt continued. "I begged her not to come to the shop today." He pointed at his chest. "I admit I need a break every bit as much as she needs to rest. But I begged her to let me do the books." He smacked the back of his right hand into the palm of his left. "But she wouldn't hear of it."

"Maybe you could take a quick break and you and I could go pick up some lunch for her."

Wyatt snapped his fingers. "That sounds like a great plan." He headed back toward the counter. Mike followed him into the office area behind the counter space. Gracie was as curled up as a nine months pregnant woman could be on the love seat. Wyatt gently closed the office door. "I'm glad she's sleeping. She doesn't rest well. I won't be able to leave now."

"You want me to pick something up for you?"

"No. I'm going to try to get the books caught up before she wakes up."

Mike chuckled. "That sounds like a good idea." He walked to the front door.

"Hey." Wyatt's voice stopped him. "Did you need anything?"

For a few moments Mike had forgotten his anxiety about the date with Lacy. And Wyatt had enough going on. He didn't need to add anything else. "No." He waved as he opened the door. The bell sounded again, and Mike hoped it didn't wake Gracie. "I'll see you later."

He headed down the sidewalk toward the Main Street Café. He preferred the diner's food, but he simply couldn't patron there again until after his and Lacy's date. As he walked down the sidewalk, he noticed a woman several yards in front of him with her head down as she rummaged through her bag.

He recognized the woman, but he couldn't quite figure out

from where. Not only was her face lowered, but the wind blew wisps of her long blond hair in front of her as well.

As the distance between them shortened, Mike wasn't sure if he should veer to the left or right. The sidewalks were too narrow. The woman hadn't looked up and she continued to walk down the center.

Mike stepped into the street to let her pass, but the woman shifted herself to the left and still bumped into him with her elbow. Hard.

"I'm so sorry." She looked up.

Mike's mouth fell open. "It's you."

Recognition wrapped her features, and she turned bright crimson. Her light-green eyes with flecks of brown seemed to flash with the deepening color of her skin.

She pulled her hand out of her bag and several items fell out. He bent down to help her retrieve them. He chuckled. "Don't bend down with me this time. My lip has only just healed."

He stood up and handed her the lip gloss and pen that had fallen in the street. Tears welled in her eyes and she stepped back. "I'm so sorry."

Before he could respond, she hurried down the sidewalk. *There must be something about me making women cry this week.*

He walked into the café. As long as it wasn't Lacy doing the crying. As anxious as he felt about their date, he looked forward to the fact that they were finally having one. He didn't want to do anything to mess it up.

three

Johanna twisted her long hair into a ball then fastened it with a clip. The morning had been quite hectic as she made sure she had everything needed for the afternoon's "Spring into a Good Book." Conveniently, the county's preschool and kindergarten was located right next to the public library. Throughout the year, the school and library joined forces to encourage literacy among the students.

Today the library hosted a fairly involved event with three stations for the children to visit. The head librarian had recruited a local farmer—Johanna believed she said the man's name was Nick—to bring a live calf for the students to see and pet. He planned to talk with them about the many duties of a farmer in the spring. Johanna would read a book to the children about the spring, and then Nick's wife, Addy, would help the children plant a seed in a small plastic cup to take home.

She tried to focus on the children who would be coming down the school's steps and over to the library's outdoor area at any moment. Instead, her mind replayed the walk down Main Street, as she'd rummaged through her purse for lunch money. She'd run into the man again. Literally.

She'd spent enough time worrying over that man. Then to run into him again? What were the chances? She knew his face would be imprinted in her mind for weeks to come. This time he hadn't looked angry. Actually, he'd seemed amused that she'd run into him a second time.

Well, she wasn't amused. She was fully humiliated. He must think her a complete klutz. The truth was she was actually quite careful and meticulous about things. She liked things to go as planned.

The school door opened and the children started toward the library. The teachers faced a challenge keeping the children from racing to the calf and the other activities. But safety came first.

Mrs. Love, the head librarian, arranged the students into groups of three and sent them to each station. One tall, dark-haired boy stuck out his bottom lip and crossed his arms in front of his chest when she pointed him toward Johanna. "I don't want to listen to her read. I want to see the baby cow."

Johanna settled the rest of the children on the quilts she'd laid out for them to sit on, while the boy became more agitated with Mrs. Love. The older woman tried to scoot him toward the quilts, but he dug his heels into the ground. "I don't want to listen to no stupid book."

"Young man." Mrs. Love placed her hand against her chest.

Knowing the older librarian had little experience with children, Johanna rushed to Mrs. Love and the boy. She knelt down to his level and rested her hand on his arm. "You know what? I really need someone to help me turn the pages of the book. Do you know anyone who could do that?"

He grunted and shook his head.

"Hmm. Well, it has to be someone who wants to learn about the springtime. Someone who one day might grow up to be one of River Run's best farmers, because he will have learned the things a farmer needs to do in the spring."

The boy's expression softened and he uncrossed his arms and raised his hand. "I want to be the best farmer in River Run."

Johanna smiled. "You do? Well, could you turn the pages for me?"

The boy nodded and grabbed hold of Johanna's hand. If the overgrown tyke pulled her heartstrings any tighter, she'd burst into tears for sure. "But I still get to see the baby cow, right?"

"You definitely still get to see her."

"Okay."

The afternoon grew hotter but the students became more inquisitive and excited about all they were learning. By the time the last group had gone through, Johanna thought she would have to take a nap on the quilts spread on the ground before she'd be able to do anything else.

Knowing that wasn't an option, she folded the quilts then walked over to Addy to help clean up the plastic cups, seeds, and soil. "Thanks for doing this today. I think the kids really enjoyed it."

Addy looked at her. "I think I had as much fun as they did." She waved her hand in front of her face. "I am a bit warm from the heat." She opened her water bottle and took a long drink. "I'm just barely past the first trimester of my pregnancy. I'm still not quite over the sickness part."

Johanna clasped her hands. "Congratulations. Then we appreciate your willingness to help out today even more."

Having already loaded the calf, Nick joined them. He placed his palm on Addy's cheek. "You look a little flushed. I think it's time for you to get home and get some rest."

Addy laughed and shook her head. She looked at Johanna. "You'd think I was fighting some kind of illness the way this man worries over me." She gazed up at her husband. "Pregnant women are supposed to get flushed, Nick."

"Well, when my pregnant woman gets flushed, I want her to rest."

Johanna felt a niggling of jealousy at the obvious love between them. That was what she longed for. Her mom and Gavin's mom kept slipping hints for the two of them, but she didn't feel that way toward her childhood friend. She wanted a man to look at her as if God had created her just for him. She wanted commitment and friendship, but she wanted more. She wanted a man who protected her and loved her with all his heart.

"I think your husband is right. You need to go on home." She swept her hand across the outdoor area. "There's very little left to do. Go home and rest." She extended her hand. "It was my pleasure to meet you, Addy." After shaking Addy's hand, she shook Nick's. "And you, too, Nick."

"It was our pleasure to meet you." Nick patted her shoulder with a strength he must not have realized he had. "I hope we'll get the chance to see you again."

She nodded, though she knew it wasn't very likely. She worked at the library in River Run, but she and her family lived about ten miles down the road in Hickory Hill. Unless the couple started visiting the library, and today was the first day she'd seen them there, she'd probably never see them again.

❧

Mike sat on the edge of his brown leather couch. He placed his elbows on top of his legs then rested his chin on his fists.

The laptop, sitting on the coffee table in front of him, was actually sticking its tongue out at him. Originally, he'd put the screensaver on there because he thought it funny. Right now, it wasn't so funny.

His article deadline loomed the next day—the same day as his date with Lacy. He'd never been late on a deadline. Not even when his brother passed away. He knew he'd been preoccupied with Drew's wedding, and he and his dad were overwhelmingly busy on the farm with spring planting, but this proved ridiculous. He had one day to write the entire article, and he still didn't even know what to write about.

He stood up and grabbed his writing fishing pole out of the corner. His buddies made fun of him for keeping the first fishing pole his dad ever bought him in the corner of his living room. But they didn't know he sometimes used it as inspiration when he struggled with an article. They didn't even know he wrote articles.

And he didn't want them to know. Nick and Drew had always been so competitive, trying to beat each other at everything from corn hole to cattle farming. They'd even made a bet about who could keep their mom's flowers alive the longest when they were kids. Being a few years younger than Drew and Nick, Mike and Wyatt never had a chance when it came to beating them.

Wyatt never did mind. He hadn't been raised on a farm, so he just enjoyed it when one of them included him. And Wyatt had spent most of every summer at Mike's house. The truth was, Mike didn't mind the losing, either. He'd found a love for words when he was no bigger than a coonhound.

Of course, he never told his friends about his adoration

for reading and writing. They'd laugh him all over the farm. It still didn't stop him from taking a few community college writing classes after high school. He never graduated from college, but he landed a job writing fishing articles for one of Kentucky's largest outdoorsman magazines. Between that and farming, he lived all he'd ever dreamed.

Except having a wife and kids.

Pushing aside the thought that caused his writer's block, he pretended to cast his old fishing pole. He'd been overpowered by so many emotions the first summer his dad had taken him fishing. In a lifetime, he didn't believe he would be able to pen all he thought and felt on that day. But every once in a while, when an article just fought him to be written, he'd pretend to cast the line and a thought or memory of some kind would surface again.

He closed his eyes and tried to envision the first fish he'd reeled up with this rod. He could still see the little bluegill. It had to be the smallest one that ever lived. But he'd been so proud. Felt so accomplished.

Keeping his eyes closed, he took several slow breaths. *Help me, Lord. I desperately need an idea.*

His cell phone rang, breaking his concentration. With a growl, he looked at the screen. The screen read his honeymooning friend's name. "Drew? Why would Drew be calling me on his honeymoon?"

Dread filled his gut. No man in his right mind would ever call a friend on his honeymoon. Unless something bad had happened. Mike didn't know if he could take any bad news. Everything in him wanted to ignore the call and try to focus on his article. But he knew there would be no focusing now.

Not until he knew Drew and Melody were safe.

He pushed the TALK button. "Hello."

"Hey. What's up, man?"

Mike swallowed the knot in his throat. Drew didn't sound distressed, but why else would he call? Mike placed the fishing pole on the couch and sat in the recliner, preparing for the worst. "Nothing's up with me. How are you?"

"I'm fine. The beach is beautiful, although not as pretty as my wife."

Mike heard Melody's soft giggle, and his body relaxed. If something were wrong they wouldn't sound so happy. Mike furrowed his brows and scratched his forehead. "Drew, why are you calling me?"

"Your date with Lacy's tomorrow, isn't it?"

"Yeah."

"I just called to tell you not to stress. Be yourself. We've been friends since before you were born. Remember how your mom says I was punching on you when you were still in her belly?"

Mike grinned. "Yeah."

"Well, I know you're probably feeling a little nervous. Overanalyzing everything like you always do."

Mike leaned back in the recliner and allowed it to rock back and forth. "So you think you know me so well?"

Drew laughed. "Am I right?"

Mike chewed the inside of his mouth and wrinkled his nose. "Maybe."

Drew's guffaw sounded over the line. "I knew I was. Look man, I'm calling you on my honeymoon. On my honeymoon!"

Mike blew out a breath. "I definitely wouldn't have asked you to do that."

"But I called you just the same to tell you that as goofy as it sounds coming from one of your best buddies, I want you to know you're a great guy. Put your shyness to the side and just be yourself with Lacy."

Mike smiled. "I really appreciate that."

Drew chuckled. "Think of it like this, you're the fisherman casting the line. If she's the fish God's prepared for you, she'll take the bait and you'll be able to reel her on up."

"Thanks, man. See you next week."

"I don't know. Melody and I may stay here forever." Her giggles sounded over the line before it went dead.

Mike mulled over Drew's words. *I've got an idea.* He looked at his old fishing pole, the first one he'd ever had. The one that conjured all sorts of childhood memories and emotions.

"There's a reason you didn't work for inspiration today." He placed the fishing pole back in its spot in the corner. "You conjure up all kinds of childlike feelings. This article's going to be about the marriage between the fisherman and his fish."

❧

Johanna drove home with the annuals she and her sisters and mother would plant the following day. As a tradition, the Smith women planted flowers the day before Mother's Day. Then Sunday they treated their mother to homemade dishes, made solely by the girls and their father, for dinner after church. This year her mother had requested all impatiens in various shades of pink and white.

She pulled into the driveway and honked the horn. Her

youngest sister ran out the front door to greet her. With Bethany having a natural green thumb, they'd learned to heed her advice about the placement of the flowers. Bethany opened the back door of the car and pulled out a flat. "These look really nice, Johanna. Where did you get them this year?"

"Well, Locklear's Greenhouse costs a bit more, but I thought they looked worth it. Besides, it's Mama's Mother's Day gift."

Bethany nodded. "You made the right choice."

Johanna looked toward the house. "Where are Mama and Amber?"

Bethany let out a sigh. "Fighting over math again."

"Ugh. You get the flowers. I'll go help." Johanna grabbed her purse and coffee mug out of the front seat and headed into the house. She petted Max then walked into the guest room they'd turned into their schoolroom.

Amber slouched forward in a chair, her eyes red from having been crying and her gaze focused on the wall in front of her. Her mother rested in the rocking chair that sat against the wall. She called it her calming chair whenever Johanna or one of her sisters pushed her patience. Mama had her head back and her eyes closed. Johanna knew she prayed for God's will with Amber.

Her sister wanted desperately to go to public high school. Outgoing and boisterous, she was the direct opposite of Johanna and Bethany. She learned best by talking and experimenting. She thrived in groups, like when they did group lessons in Sunday school.

"I'm just dumb." Amber's words were flat, and she continued to stare at the wall in front of her.

"Amber, you are not dumb. Don't say such things." Johanna sat in the chair beside Amber's desk. "You just struggle with math. We all struggle with something."

Amber peered at Johanna. "What do you struggle with?"

Johanna swallowed. "You know what, I didn't struggle with academics. But I struggle a lot with talking to people. You know how shy I am with people I don't know." She nudged her sister. "But you, you're naturally friendly and outgoing."

"A lot of good it does me cooped up in a house with my parents and sisters all day."

Johanna pushed a strand of hair behind her ear. She hadn't meant for the conversation to shift to Amber's desire to go to high school. She tried a different angle. "You're also the most musically talented person I know. Amber, yours is undeniably a true gift from God."

"And one I can only share with the people in my family and in my church because I am not allowed to experience anything of the world."

Johanna gazed back at her mother. Mama had opened her eyes. She wasn't angry with Amber's words. Instead, her expression etched one of true concern, of true openness to whatever God wanted for her middle daughter.

Johanna looked back at her sister. "Amber, I do not believe it is Mama's and Daddy's intention to shelter us from the world. Yes, they mean to protect and teach us what the Bible says, but look at me. Your most bashful sister works at a public library. Granted, people do not surround me every day, but you know I feel much more at home simply basking in God's nature, without speaking with anyone for hours at a time."

Amber faced her sister. Johanna's heart wanted to break in two at the anguish in her sister's expression.

"But I do need to be around people. I want to share my gift of music with everyone I meet. I want to go away to college to learn to be even better at my talent." She looked back at the wall. "All of that won't even matter if I can't understand math. I won't be able to go to college anyway."

Johanna felt her mother get out of the seat from behind them. She placed a hand on Amber's shoulder. "Go on upstairs and wash up."

Amber nodded then stood and left the room.

Johanna turned toward her mother. "Mama—"

Her mother shook her head to silence her. "Supper is almost done in the slow cooker. Why don't you head on out to your favorite spot at the pond and pray that your daddy and I make the best choice for Amber. I'll be up in my room doing the same."

Johanna nodded. She walked into the kitchen and grabbed a water bottle out of the refrigerator. She opened the back door and Max followed her outside and up the hill that led to the pond.

She sat on the bench and lifted her face toward the heavens. She prayed fervently for her sister and that God would give her parents wisdom. Amber was so different than Johanna or Bethany. But Johanna wondered if she was really a lot like their father. Before he'd married their mother, he'd been a traveling preacher, sharing God's good news all over the southern parts of Kentucky and into Tennessee and West Virginia. She petitioned God once more to make His will for Amber transparent to her parents.

Looking back down at the calm waters, she noticed a small frog hop from beneath a leaf and closer to the water. She chuckled at the remembrances of the many times she'd caught frogs and taken them home as pets. Much to her mother's chagrin. "I think I'll let you stay at your own home," she whispered to the creature.

Her stomach growled and she pressed her hand against it. "I think it's time I get home to mine as well."

four

His big date with Lacy had finally arrived. Mike exhaled a long breath as she waited for him to open the passenger's door for her. At first he'd planned to see if his dad would let him borrow their car, as Mike only had a truck. But he still hadn't told his parents about the date. He wanted to see how the night went first. When she struggled to hold down her skirt and still lift herself into the cab, he berated himself for not asking.

Nervous, he shut the door too fast and almost caught her fingers. He closed his eyes before walking around the truck to the driver's side. *Calm my nerves, Lord.*

The most bashful of his friends, Mike was known for doing clumsy things when he was nervous. A vision of the woman who'd bumped into him at the wedding and on the sidewalk popped into his head. He shook the thought away. Why would he think of her at this moment?

He hopped in and started the truck. Accidentally putting the gear in neutral instead of reverse, Mike quickly fixed his error and backed out of her driveway.

Lacy crossed her legs and shifted to face him. "So, where are we going?"

"I thought we'd go to"—his voice squeaked, and Mike cleared his throat—"to Lexington. You could pick out a restaurant from there."

She mentioned a Mexican restaurant. He'd heard it was a good restaurant, but he hated Mexican food. In fact, it was his least favorite. He also noticed Lacy didn't bother to ask him if he liked it. It seemed a bit insensitive to him, but he'd never really dated before so maybe he was wrong. He turned toward her. "Did you have to work today?"

"Yes, and I worked with Sarah. She drives me absolutely crazy. First, you have to fight her to keep her hairnet on. I mean, *hello*, people don't want your scraggly red hair in their food. Then, she always takes too long on her breaks. She leaves me to cover for her for like half an hour, then she gets all upset if I take the tip for the tables she's left stranded all that time."

Mike grew more uncomfortable as Lacy continued to talk about the people she worked with. All the things she said may be true, but he didn't think it was appropriate for her to be sharing them with him.

He pulled into the restaurant's parking lot and they walked inside. The dark room and blaring Latino music led him to believe they wouldn't be able to have any kind of conversation. But it was the smell that almost sent him running back outside.

After taking a deep breath, he left his name with the hostess and took a pager. The restaurant entryway was packed so they weren't able to sit together. Lacy sat on the bench close to the hostess, while Mike stood back by the door.

He looked through the menu the hostess had given them for the least spicy dish he could find. It appeared his best bet would be the tacos. Maybe this time they wouldn't give him indigestion as they had every other time he'd ever eaten them.

As the minutes continued to pass, Mike looked around the room at the burnt orange and green painted walls. Mexican blankets and paintings and sombreros hung from the walls, with a multicolored light of some kind above each table and booth. The colors were very festive, but the music was simply too loud. He could already feel a headache tapping at the front of his forehead with the beat of the drum.

He looked at his watch. They'd been waiting for thirty minutes, and it didn't seem anyone had been seated. He peered at Lacy. She seemed deep in conversation with the older woman sitting beside her.

He studied the woman he'd been so taken with for so many years. Her long brown hair was beautiful. It was sleek and straight and shone beneath the lights. Her facial features were dainty. All of them—eyes, nose, mouth, even her chin. She wore glasses, which really added to her features. She was a very pretty woman. It was the reason he'd been so attracted to her, but their conversation in the truck had taken him by surprise. Her features had twisted into an unattractiveness he'd not expected each time she spoke poorly of someone else.

He watched as Lacy leaned closer to the older woman and whispered something in her ear. The woman looked around Lacy and up at the hostess. She pursed her lips and nodded as she focused her attention back on Lacy. His date wrinkled her nose then opened her mouth and placed her finger inside in a gagging motion.

Mike looked up at the hostess. What could Lacy have

been belittling her for? By the look on the woman's face, he believed she'd heard whatever Lacy said. Lacy was not the woman Mike thought she was.

Unable to take any more of the music, the smell, and most importantly the rudeness of his date, Mike took the pager back to the hostess. "Please mark McCauley off the list."

The woman frowned. "I'm sorry the wait is taking so long."

Lacy stood and peered at the woman. "If this restaurant were better staffed, it would—"

Mike lifted his hand to keep Lacy from saying anything further. He pulled some money from his wallet and handed it to the woman. "You're working very hard, and I appreciate your efforts. I hope no one has said or done anything that would make you feel otherwise."

The woman blushed, and Mike felt heat rise up his own neck and cheeks. He'd pushed aside his shyness so much in the last few weeks that he feared it was starting to get the best of him. Either that or the smell of the food finally made him sick.

He knew Lacy stood fuming beside him, but he didn't care. The woman had been nothing that Mike thought. Possibly Mike had dreamed her into something she wasn't. At the diner, when she waited his table, she'd always seemed so kind. Now, he wondered if her irritations with Drew were proof of her true character. *I have to admit Drew can definitely irritate the most rational of people.*

With all the gentleness he could muster, he grabbed Lacy's elbow and walked out of the restaurant with her. She didn't say a word as he opened the passenger's door. Shutting the door behind her, he walked around to the driver's side. *God, give me grace to speak with humility and truth.*

After hopping in the cab, he started the truck. "I'm ready to head on home, but I'd love to buy you something from a drive-through. I know you must be hungry."

Lacy crossed her arms in front of her chest. She stared at him with all the contempt he expected. "What is going on, Mike?"

Her words sounded hateful and furious, and Mike knew he needed to be careful with everything he said. He cleared his throat. "Did that hostess do anything to upset you?"

She glared at him. "What are you talking about?"

"I saw you talking about her with the older woman. I wondered what the hostess did."

"You were on the other side of the room. You have no idea what we were saying."

Stealing his gaze away from the road for just a moment, he peered at her. "It was obvious by your gagging motion that you were unhappy with her. That woman didn't deserve that."

Lacy leaned back against the seat. He couldn't see the steam rolling out of her ears and off the top of her head, but he felt confident that if it were possible, it would have been there. After several moments of silence, Lacy growled, "I cannot believe you would talk to me like that."

"Lacy, I can't believe you talked about your colleagues the way you did. It was embarrassing, and it made me feel uncomfortable. I don't need to hear such negative things about those people."

Lacy shifted in her seat. "Well, don't you just think you're Mr. Perfect. I didn't mean to burn your ears by the things I said."

"From everything I knew about you at the diner, I thought you were a Christian woman, a—"

"Are you judging my faith?"

Mike looked at her. "I guess I am questioning it."

Lacy sucked in her breath and looked out the passenger's window. Mike chewed his bottom lip. *Was that too much, Lord? That didn't feel like humility, even if it was truth.*

She'd never suggested a fast-food restaurant, and Mike had been too upset to offer again. With only a few miles to Lacy's house, Mike continued to pray that God would guide his parting words. He didn't want to be mean to Lacy, but he didn't want to be a part of her gossip, either.

He pulled into her driveway and turned off the ignition. Before he could get out, she opened the door. Mike reached for her arm, but she shrugged him away. "I don't mean to hurt your feelings, Lacy. I only want to be honest about. . ."

She hopped out of the truck and glared at him. "Thanks for nothing, Mike." Then she slammed the door.

❧

Johanna snuggled into her bed. It had been a long day of planting flowers and baking homemade bread for all the mothers in their church family for Mother's Day. It had been a week since she'd been able to catch up on her favorite magazines.

As a lover of God's creation and an avid outdoorswoman, she devoured several magazines each month. Probably one of her favorites was the Kentucky-based fishing magazine that had gained a nationwide following. One of her favorite writers, or maybe he just intrigued her the most, was John James.

Whenever she read his articles, she always felt he wrote

about River Run, and sometimes even Hickory Hill. It stood to reason a lot of places mentioned within its pages might seem like her hometown. But the descriptions in his articles sounded as if the author was someone from their area, someone who enjoyed the same places where she loved to bask in God's glory.

In her mind, she envisioned an older man, probably around five feet, six inches. He'd have a bushy white beard and wear an aged brown fishing hat. His eyebrows would be as bushy as his beard and his deep-blue eyes would mimic the color of a clear stream. He had a ready word of encouragement and a quick smile, and could easily be the grandfather of every child who'd ever wanted to learn to fish.

She found his newest article in the magazine. An oversize, cartoon, smallmouth bass seemed to swim right off the page and toward a hook. She'd love to meet John James one day and find out if she was right about him.

She read the article he'd written about smallmouth bass. Every time she finished his writings, she always felt like a young girl on her first trip to the fishing pond with her mom. Something about the way he said and placed his words always brought back nostalgic feelings of childhood. She wondered if that was the reason she liked his writing so much. He wrote with pure innocence.

With her eyes growing heavy, she shut the magazine and placed it on the floor beside her bed. The distant sound of thunder lifted her lids. She looked at her bedroom door. Sure enough, Max stood in the doorway with his head lowered. The silly dog was terrified of storms. She patted the bed. "All right. Come on."

Max jumped onto the foot of the bed, and Johanna shook her head as the dog whimpered until she pressed her leg against his back. "You're such a chicken, Max."

Johanna looked at the bedroom door again. Max wouldn't be the last visitor for the night. Just as she expected, Amber stood in the doorway. She shrugged and ducked her head. "It's getting ready to storm."

"I know." She patted the empty side of her bed, thankful her parents had given her their old queen-size one.

She glanced back toward the door. Sometimes, if Bethany were already asleep, a storm wouldn't wake her. Her figure appeared in the doorway. Tonight wasn't one of those nights. Johanna laughed. "Come on, Bethany. We'll make room."

Bethany settled in between her big sisters. After several shiftings, Johanna situated her legs to satisfy Max's need to have his back pressed against someone.

The room grew quiet except the occasional roll of thunder. Then Johanna heard the faint, muffled giggles from the room across the hall. She knew her parents found it hilarious that everyone got in bed with her when it stormed. Unable to resist, Johanna yelled, "Mom, Dad, I think I'm scared. I'm going to come in there and get in bed with you. Mine's too crowded."

"Oh, no you're not." Her mother laughed.

"You and Amber and Bethany and Max can all stay together in your room," her father added.

Her sisters broke out into giggles once more and it took several minutes for the whole family to settle back down. Once they did, Johanna watched her bedroom window. As a second-story bedroom, only a thin curtain covered her window, and she could see the occasional flash of lightning.

Unlike her sisters, she enjoyed the storms. She always envisioned them as God's way of communicating with the earth and sky. He commanded His creation what He wanted, and when and how He wanted it done. She knew it was silly, just as believing thunder was God knocking down pins while bowling was silly. But she enjoyed storms anyway. They showed God's awesome majesty.

A flash of lightning and a clap of thunder sounded right outside the house, causing her to jump. Without a doubt, she served an awesome God.

five

Mike woke up Monday morning with a heavy heart. He'd spent most of the day before with his mom and dad. It had been a hard day, being the first Mother's Day since Joe's death. He and his father had attended church, as they did every Sunday, without his mother. Then afterward, they took her to lunch.

In years past, they would drive to Lexington and take her to the mall to pick out a new summer dress. He and Joe, and if truth be told, their father, viewed it as the most sacrificial, painful task they could do for their mother. This year she refused to go, saying she didn't have anywhere to wear a new dress. He missed the shopping trip. It broke his heart to see his mother carry so much bitterness.

But it wasn't just his mother that had him feeling blue. He continued to dwell on his date with Lacy on Saturday. How could he have been so wrong about her? He'd spent years fawning after her at the diner. He should have been paying attention to who she was as a person and not just that she was a pretty waitress. *God, I've been looking at her superficially, and I know better than that.*

Trying to push the gloom to the back of his mind, he put on his work clothes. Looking outside the window, he noted the looming dark clouds and a good wind blowing the treetops. Looked like a rainy day was about to set in. That was all he needed.

He forced himself to perk up. They did need a good rain. A good, daylong, steady one. Just because he felt a little down didn't mean he needed to be taking it out on the weather. He picked up his ball cap and put it on his head. "Enough of this whining. It's time to head to the farm. Mom will have breakfast ready."

Two years ago he'd bought the old farmhouse and property that backed up to his family's farm. He'd had to do a lot of work to it. Put in a new toilet and shower. Had to tear up the existing floor and lay tile and hardwood. It still wasn't fit for a family, as it needed more insulation and new windows so it would be cooler in the summer and warmer in the winter, but it allowed him to be on his own and still farm with his father.

A drizzle started when he got in his pickup. By the time he'd reached his parents' house, a steady rain fell from the sky. He ran up to the porch and wiped his boots on the front mat, lifted his ball cap off his head, and brushed the raindrops off his shirt. Sucking in a deep breath to prepare for his mother's doldrums, he opened the front door. "Steady rain outside."

"We need it," his father called from the kitchen.

He joined his father in the kitchen and saw his mother standing at the sink, staring out the window. "Not so many years ago, you boys would have been out there getting all wet and muddy, and I'd be hollering at you to come inside."

His mother's voice was low, little more than a whisper. The pain she felt seeped through every syllable. He wished he could help her. She was already taking medicine. Though his father didn't say it outright, Mike knew his dad monitored how much she took.

Mike wanted to shake his mother, to poke into her head

that she would never come out of this depression until she allowed God to heal her heart. But she was still so mad at God for taking her son.

He and his father had grieved as well. Grieved miserably. Still grieved at times. But they sought God's healing. It was his own father who reminded him once that God understood the pain they felt. That His Son had paid the ultimate price for our sins. Tears had streamed down his dad's cheeks at the realization that God truly understood his pain. Mike would never forget that conversation. He'd never before known such admiration and respect for his father's strength through Christ.

"Mom, the bacon smells wonderful." Trying to change the subject, Mike sat down beside his father at the table. He picked up several pieces and put them on the plate his mother had already set out for him. He scooped up a spoonful of scrambled eggs then grabbed a couple of biscuits out of a bowl. "Would you mind to bring me some coffee?"

His mother turned away from the window and smiled at him. "Sure."

His mother was naturally hospitable, and he'd learned as a little boy that nothing pleased her more than to take care of her sons. She grabbed the pot off the coffeemaker and poured the hot liquid into a mug. The smile that didn't quite reach her eyes remained on her face until she placed the coffee in front of him then sat down beside his father.

He noticed she stared at the mug she'd given him. He looked at it and realized it was the one with a picture Joe had drawn in elementary school. This one had a stick figure of Joe with the mutt dog they'd had when he was in first grade. The little rascal had gotten out one day, ventured onto their country road, and was struck and killed by one of their neighbors. Joe had cried for two weeks straight.

Mike looked up at his mother. She placed her elbow on the table then cupped her hand over her forehead. After a moment, she rubbed her hand across her face. "I think I'm going to go lie down for a bit."

She stood, and Mike watched as she left the room. "Not a good day today, huh?"

Mike studied his father as he shook his head. His dad had aged since Joe's passing. His dark hair was now streaked with more gray than brown. Deep bags darkened his eyes. He'd lost weight as well.

His dad sucked in a deep breath. "Nope. It's not going to be a good day for your mother." He filled his coffee cup with the pot Mike's mother had left on the table. He sat all the way back in his chair. "So, tell me what's been going on."

Mike shrugged. "Nothing much. Working the farm and writing articles. Same as always."

His dad shook his head and made a loud hissing noise as he sucked air between his two front teeth. "No. Something else is going on."

Mike wrapped his hands around the coffee mug, enjoying the warmth of the brew. He had no intention of burdening his father with his inner struggle over Lacy or the fact that he was the biggest loser of all his friends. He sounded whiny in his own ears. He surely didn't want to add any more silliness to all his father had to deal with. He looked at his father but couldn't quite make contact with his eyes as he said, "Everything's fine."

His dad sat forward. "Boy, I thought I taught you better than to lie to me." He grabbed a piece of bacon and crunched a bite out of it. "Now, tell me the truth."

Mike grinned at his father. He may have been spending every day of the last several months with the stress he'd feel with a two-year drought, but he still paid attention to what was going on with Mike. It was one of the things he loved about his father. One of the things he hoped he would be able to show to his own children one day. "There's no getting anything past you, is there?"

"Nope. As long as there's breath in this old man's body"— he said, pointing to his chest—"I'm going to be involved in your life."

Mike couldn't hold back the chuckle at his father's words. They sounded familiar, as they were the same ones he'd said throughout his teenage years when Mike rebelled in some form or fashion. "All right. I might as well start at the beginning." He pointed to the window. Rain streamed down as if being poured straight down from buckets in the sky. "Looks like we have a minute."

His dad nodded. "God knows when a good rain's needed."

Mike chewed on the wisdom of his father's words. He scratched his jaw, noting a spot he'd missed shaving. "A long time ago, Wyatt, Nick, Drew, and I made a bet."

"The no-women bet."

Mike gaped at his dad. "How did you know about it?"

"Son, everyone in town knew about it. I thought it was quite funny. Knew it wouldn't last long, but I still thought it was humorous."

Mike peered at his father. He wondered how many things

the old man knew about. He thought of the times he and his buddies went mudding without permission, and the one time in particular when they'd busted the radiator. Luckily, Drew had been able to figure out how to fix it.

His father crossed his legs. "Now don't be worrying about all the things I know or don't know. Go on."

Mike rubbed his temple. "I'd always thought it was a kind of stupid bet. I'm not really as competitive as the other guys, but it was supposed to be just for fun, and I always lose anyway. Well. . ." He paused for a moment. "I guess this time I wanted to lose."

"But you're the winner."

Mike smacked his thigh. "I know. Doesn't that beat all? The first thing I actually do win I never wanted to."

"So how does Lacy come into all this?"

"Dad." Mike placed his elbows on the table and leaned closer to his father. "How could you possibly know about Lacy?"

"I told you I'm keeping tabs. So, how did the date go?"

Mike decided it wasn't worth it to ask how his father knew about their date Saturday night. He might as well just tell him how it went. "It was awful. She's not the woman I thought she was." Mike's cheeks warmed. "Even as I say that I feel wrong to say anything bad about her to you, and yet foolish that I've liked the woman for so long."

"Hmm. Son, it's good you went out with Lacy. Now you know she's not the woman God has for you."

"I know." Mike sat back in his seat again. He looked at the empty bowl that had been full of biscuits earlier.

"Then what's the matter?"

"I shouldn't have been spending all that time pining over her. I should have just asked her out three years ago and figured it out then."

His dad placed his elbows on the table and clasped his hands. "Son, you've changed so much in the last three years, especially since your brother passed away. Maybe you weren't ready to go out with her then. Maybe you wouldn't have been as in tune to what God wants for you—until now."

His dad pushed away from the table and stood. "The rain's settling down. You wanna clean up the kitchen for Mom or go check on the animals?"

Knowing how much his father detested doing dishes, Mike said, "I'll clean up and meet you out there in a few minutes."

He thought about his father's words as he rinsed off the dishes and placed them in the dishwasher. His faith had grown since his brother passed. And though he was still naturally shy, he knew he was more confident than he'd ever been and more willing to stand up for what was right. *God, You know what You want for my life, and Dad is right, You've grown me up a lot in the last few years. I still want a wife. I want all that I see my friends have. I ask You to bring me one. The right one.*

❧

Johanna hefted her purse higher on her shoulder then raced into the grocery store. Today was Amber's seventeenth birthday and she'd promised her sister she'd make her a chocolate crème pie from scratch.

But the day had not started well. First, her boss phoned asking her to come in for the morning because one of the workers called in sick. Knowing Mrs. Love would be shorthanded with the monthly women's book club meeting at ten, she simply couldn't decline. Thankfully, she'd had the presence of mind to place the ingredients for Amber's pie on the counter. Which was how she discovered they were out of cocoa. She couldn't believe it, they were never out of cocoa.

Johanna looked at her watch. It was 1:30. Her mother had invited several families from church over at 5:30. Johanna was really going to have to rush to get the pie finished before then. Not to mention she had to run into River Run's grocery store, one she was not familiar with.

Peering down at the list of items her mother asked her to pick up, "since you have to go anyway," she grabbed a cart and headed toward the aisle with the baking ingredients sign above it.

Thankfully, the store was almost empty, so she found potato chips and plastic cups with relative ease. Her cell phone rang. She pulled it out of her purse and pushed the TALK button.

Her mother's voice sounded through the line. "Are you still at the store?"

"Yes."

"Go ahead and pick up a couple of two-liters of something diet. I thought I had some, but I can't find them."

Johanna glanced at her watch again. It wasn't her mother's fault she'd been called in to work that morning. But with each minute that passed Johanna feared she wouldn't be able to finish the pie her sister had requested practically every day for the last month. "Okay. I'll be home soon."

She pushed the END button and looked at the signs above

the aisles for soft drinks. Spying them, she rushed toward the aisle. *I think I might have a coupon.*

She continued to walk as she rummaged through her purse. Her cart jolted. She looked and saw she'd bumped into someone. Someone wearing tennis shoes. Which probably meant the back of his ankles would really hurt. "I'm so sorry."

The man lifted his right foot a bit as he turned to face her. "No prob— You?"

It couldn't be. It simply was not possible. There stood the same man she'd run into at the barn and on the sidewalk. She was normally a very careful person, but it seemed as if some weird force propelled her to wound this man in some way.

Her cheeks warmed and her hands shook slightly until she gripped the cart handle. "I—I don't know what to say."

A smile bowed the man's lips, and Johanna couldn't help but admit how cute he was. He extended his hand. "I think I'd better introduce myself to you before you need to notify my family."

Johanna frowned. "Notify your family?"

"Yeah. The next time you run into me you may put me in the hospital."

A new wave of warmth washed over Johanna's face and neck, but she reached and accepted the man's handshake. Her heart raced when their hands touched. She shook hands with plenty of men at church, but never with the reaction this one evoked.

He tipped his head. "Mike McCauley."

"Hi. I'm Johanna Smith."

He motioned toward her cart. "You getting ready for a picnic?"

Johanna swallowed back the knot in her throat. She seemed to have lost all the saliva in her mouth as well. "It's my sister's seventeenth birthday. We're having a cookout with our church family."

He raised one eyebrow, and Johanna noted again how beautiful his blue-green eyes were. They reminded her of the sky and grass all wrapped up into one gorgeous color. Unsure what to do, she continued, "My sister wanted me to make her a chocolate crème pie, and we didn't have any cocoa." She pointed to the container in the cart. "Then Mama asked me to pick up a few things. And now I barely have time to get home and get the pie made."

Yet another wave of heat washed over her. Only this time, a cold sweat added itself to her nervousness. She gripped the cart handle until her knuckles turned white. Needing to get out of there, she nodded. "I'll see you later." She furrowed her eyebrows. "I'm sure you don't want to see me later. I mean— well—bye."

Johanna rushed to the checkout line. God blessed her with an empty lane, and she was able to pay for the groceries quickly. Pushing the cart outside, she inhaled the warm fresh air and allowed the breeze to calm her.

God, that was so embarrassing. That man must think I'm a complete idiot.

He wasn't just "that man." She knew his name now. "Mike McCauley," she whispered.

Getting his face out of her thoughts would be impossible now. Plus she had the sound of his voice to add to her thinking. This time she noticed he wasn't wearing a wedding ring. Not the groom at the wedding.

Johanna Smith, what are you thinking? she inwardly chastised herself. Opening the trunk of her car and placing the bags inside, she shut it then walked the cart to the cart rack. With just over three hours to get home, make the pie, and help her mother with the cookout, she needed to focus on Amber's birthday.

Sliding into the front seat of the car, she looked in her rearview mirror and saw a mother cradling an infant with one arm and holding the hand of a toddler with her other hand. The little guy tripped and fell forward without bracing his fall. She hopped out of the car to volunteer her help. She couldn't stand to see a child hurt.

six

Mike walked out of the grocery store and saw Johanna jump out of a car and rush to a woman holding a baby. Once he pushed his cart closer to his truck, he could see the woman also had a small boy with her. He must have fallen because Johanna bent down and helped the little guy up.

The boy's screams pealed through the parking lot, and Mike saw a scrape on his chin. The boy held his palms up to Johanna and his mother, and Mike knew he probably hurt his hands, too.

He heard Johanna say, "I have a first aid kit in my car."

He knew he was being nosy, but he watched as Johanna scooped the boy into her arms and walked to the car. The boy was too focused on his wounds to fight off the stranger who'd picked him up. The woman, who now looked on the verge of tears herself, followed Johanna to the car.

"It's so hard to try to bring both of them to the store, but my husband works double shifts a lot," the woman said as her voice cracked.

"I'm sure it's very difficult." Johanna's voice was calm. "We'll have him all fixed up in a second."

Mike watched as Johanna, still holding the screaming child, dug into the glove compartment and pulled out a large baggie of various first aid supplies.

"It's okay. We're going to make it all better. What's your name, big guy?"

"His name is Henry." The mother bounced the baby while Johanna opened a few packages of cleansing wipes.

"There now, Henry," Johanna cooed at the child as she wiped his wounds. He screamed and fought, but Johanna remained calm and continued to murmur to him in a soothing tone.

The baby in the woman's arms began to cry, and the woman grabbed a pacifier from her pocket and put it in the baby's mouth. "It's okay, sweetie." She began to bounce the baby more fervently and rocked from side to side.

"Now, this will make it feel better." Johanna opened some cream and applied it to his chin, hands, and knees. His cries shifted to whimpers when she pulled out some kind of cartoon bandages.

A few times the boy actually cackled over his whimpers when she put the brightly colored plastic strips on his hands. Johanna glanced at the mother. "Do you need some help getting your things from the store?"

"No." The woman shook her head, but Mike could tell she was shaken and overwhelmed. "I'll be fine."

"Why don't you let me help you? I don't have anything in my trunk that will ruin."

The woman sighed and smiled. "I'd really appreciate it."

Mike watched as Johanna grabbed her purse out of her car. She looked his way, and he averted his gaze. He knew she'd seen him, though.

Sneaking another peek, he watched as she carried the boy and followed the woman into the store. He knew she was in a hurry. Making a chocolate crème pie for her sister's birthday. But she'd taken time she didn't have to help out the harried mother.

He hopped into the truck cab and turned the ignition. *God, are You trying to tell me something? Is that why she keeps bumping into me?*

⊷

Johanna didn't get home until almost four. Thankfully, her father had come home from work early and helped with the food preparation. Her sisters had cleaned the house spotless, and she would have just enough time to fix her sister's pie. A warm pie tasted better than a cold one anyway.

She tried to focus on the ingredients for the dessert but her mind kept drifting back to running into Mike at the grocery. He seemed much kinder than her first impression, and she could no longer deny the attraction she felt.

When she saw him in the parking lot, watching her—she whipped the meringue for the top of the pie with more fervor. She'd never felt so queasy inside.

Her mother walked up behind her and said, "Gavin and his family will be here in just a bit. I believe chocolate meringue is his favorite also."

Johanna nodded but didn't say anything in response. Her mother had been dropping more hints than usual, and it made Johanna anxious. She wanted to be herself around Gavin. The way they'd been for as long as she could remember.

They'd dug out earthworms for bait together, fished together, gone gigging together. She even shot her first buck on a trip with Gavin and their fathers.

I can't even think of Gavin as a husband.

She tried to envision what it would be like to kiss her playpen pal, as they used to call each other. She wrinkled her nose at the thought then a vision of kissing Mike McCauley popped into her mind. Heat warmed her cheeks at how much she liked the idea. *God, I know nothing about this man. Or about kissing. Forgive me for these ridiculous thoughts.*

"What do you think?"

Amber's voice interrupted her thoughts. She looked at her sister who had her hands on her hips. Amber made a sweeping motion from her shoulders to her knees. The bright-pink-and-white capris outfit suited her sister to perfection. Johanna clapped. "You look absolutely gorgeous."

"And I can finally wear makeup." Amber walked closer to her and batted her eyelashes.

Several of the younger girls at their small church were already allowed to wear makeup. Her daddy detested it and wouldn't allow his daughters to wear makeup until they turned seventeen, and only as long as they wore it sparingly. "It looks really good. You did it very tastefully. Your eyes look more green than I've ever seen them."

Amber giggled. "Mama helped, of course."

Johanna hugged her younger sister. As excited as she was now, Johanna couldn't imagine what Amber would do when she found out Mama and Daddy had decided to enroll her in public high school after all.

Amber sneaked her finger into the chocolate part of the pie, and Johanna gently swatted it. "Amber, it's not finished yet."

Amber shrugged as she stuck her finger in her mouth. "Mmm. Tastes so good. And it is my birthday."

A car sounded in the driveway, and Amber jumped. People were starting to arrive. She patted Johanna's arm. "I'm so excited."

She raced out of the kitchen, and Johanna quickly folded

the meringue onto the top of the pie. She put it on a cookie sheet and placed it in the oven. It would be ready in fifteen minutes. She wiped her hands on a kitchen towel and walked out the back door to welcome whomever had arrived.

It was the Mitchell family. One boy after another unloaded from the van. Mrs. Mitchell had a son every three to four years from the time twenty-one-year-old Gavin was born all the way down to their newest six-month-old addition. All boys.

Johanna couldn't help but feel a bit sorry for the frazzled woman. The boys were all healthy and strong and helped their father on the farm, but that left little-to-no help for her. And lots more work.

Amber already stood beside the van, ready to take the youngest Mitchell boy from his car seat. She loved children as much as she loved music, and Johanna knew one day her sister would make a wonderful mother.

Gavin slipped out of the van, unbuckled the baby, and handed him to Amber. She smiled up at him, and for a moment, Johanna wondered if Gavin and Amber would be a good match when she got older. When the idea didn't bother her, Johanna knew Gavin was not, could not, be the man for her. Though she never wanted to be a jealous person, she still would need to have some inkling of concern if she thought of the man she loved with another woman.

No. Gavin was her friend. She did love him, but not in the way her mom wished. When the time was right, she would have to talk with her mother.

Johanna looked down and realized she hadn't changed since she'd gotten home. Still wearing the long black slacks and blue blouse she'd worn to the library that morning, she needed something different to wear. After eating, they'd be playing corn hole and croquet.

After getting the pie out of the oven, she ran upstairs and pulled a pair of denim capris and a T-shirt out of her dresser drawer and put them on. She heard her name from outside the window, and she peered outside to see her mother talking to Gavin. She listened carefully as her mother said, "Johanna made a chocolate meringue pie. It's your favorite, isn't it?"

"Yes, ma'am," he responded.

"Well, I'll be sure. . ."

Johanna could take it no longer. She stuck her head out the window and yelled as sweetly as she could muster. "Mama, could I see you a minute?"

Her mom gasped as she looked up at Johanna. "What are you doing upstairs, dear? We have company."

"I just need you for a moment, Mama."

Johanna watched as her mother headed toward the back door. She waved at Gavin. He smiled up at her and winked. Again, she couldn't figure out if he was just being her friend, as he'd always been, or if he was looking for something more. Those thoughts would have never even entered her mind if her mother hadn't placed them there. She hated feeling so weird around Gavin.

She paced back and forth in front of her bed as she waited for her mother to come up the stairs. *God, show me how to say this to Mama in the right way. She's got to stop. It's not fair to me or to him. Lord, it's just not fair. And I need her to listen to me. Not to brush me off. God. . .*

"Yes, Johanna, what is it? Why are you hidden up here in your room instead of with our guests?"

Johanna studied her mother. The woman looked so much younger than her forty years. Many people often thought they were sisters when they first met them. It used to drive Johanna crazy until someone mentioned that possibly God would bless her with the look-young-forever gene as well.

Her mother lived the life Johanna yearned for. She was a wife and mother. She tended an herbal and a vegetable garden, cared for strawberries and fruit trees. She loved to fish and hunt, all the things Johanna wanted out of life. And Johanna could have them with Gavin if he offered, but she'd be missing the one thing she wanted the most. She didn't look at Gavin the way Mama looked at Daddy. She didn't love him. Somehow, she had to get her mother to see that.

"Mama, I came up here to change clothes." She lifted her chin. "I heard you talking to Gavin."

Her mother frowned. "I said nothing wrong to Gavin." She swatted at the air. "I merely told him that you'd made the pie and that—"

"Mama, stop it."

Her mother looked at her.

"Please." Johanna sat on the edge of the bed. "Mama, I don't feel toward Gavin the way you'd like me to feel."

"Gavin is a good match for you."

"He's perfect." Johanna looked up at her mother, who started to smile. "But I don't love him."

Her mother shook her head. "I have told you that marriage is about friendship and commitment—"

"But it's also about love. I want what you and Daddy have."

With a heavy sigh, her mother lowered into the sitting chair beside the door. "We didn't always have love, Johanna."

Johanna sat forward, studying her mother's face. What was she saying? Johanna had just assumed her parents had fallen in love as teens and had been in love ever since. "What are you saying, Mama?"

Her mother let out a deep breath. "When I was a young woman, I was in love. But it was with another man."

Johanna swallowed the knot in her throat and gaped at her mother. "What?"

Her mother nodded. "I was. The man's name was Jimmy." She looked into Johanna's eyes, and Johanna knew it hurt her mother to talk about it. But she had to know, had to hear what her mother was about to say.

"Jimmy really liked me, but I wasn't the only girl he liked. And after dating me for six months, Jimmy decided to marry the other girl. The girl I didn't even know had existed all that time."

Her mother stood and started to pace. "I was devastated. I couldn't eat. I couldn't sleep. I couldn't do anything. Your grandparents were worried sick about me."

She wrung her hands together. "Of course you know your father met me in Tennessee. It's where all of my family is from. Well, when Jimmy finally did marry the girl, I went into an even deeper depression."

She sat on the edge of the bed beside Johanna. "Then a traveling preacher came through our town. He was kind to me and prayed for me and with me. I knew he cared for me more than I cared for him."

Her mother averted her gaze, and Johanna tried to make sense of what her mother tried to tell her.

"When he asked me to marry him"—her mother closed

her eyes—"in my heart, I knew I didn't love him. I just needed to get away from Jimmy."

"You married Daddy to get away from someone else?"

Her mother stood again. "I'm so ashamed of the way I behaved back then. What I felt for Jimmy wasn't true love, it was selfishness and my desire to have what I wanted. Your daddy knew I struggled with my feelings, but he loved me and was patient with me and when you came along—"

"You still didn't love Daddy even after I was born?"

Her mother walked over to her and wrapped her arm around Johanna's shoulders. "It took awhile, honey. That's why I know exactly what I'm talking about when I tell you marriage is about commitment and friendship. I love your daddy with a love that can only be explained by God. But I do love him."

Her mother kissed the top of her head. "Think about what I've said for a minute, but not too long. Amber will want you to be with her for her party."

Johanna stared at the window as her mother left the room. She could hardly believe what Mama had told her. She hadn't loved her daddy when they married. It was a love like theirs that she longed for.

She walked to the window and peered outside at Gavin playing corn hole with his dad, her father, and one of his younger brothers. He'd always been such a good friend. Maybe she was wrong not to believe she could love him.

Again, Mike McCauley's face flashed through her mind. She didn't even know the man. She had no reason to think about him as much as she did. *God, I'm just going to go outside and enjoy my sister's birthday. I'm leaving all the love stuff to*

You. She chuckled. *For right now. You know I'm probably going to bother You about it again later.*

Johanna joined her family outside. No matter where he went, she couldn't help but watch Gavin. She still didn't feel any kind of love for him, but she wondered if she could.

"It's time for presents," her father announced, and Amber squealed.

Their friends and family gathered around the folding table her father had set up in the backyard under the large oak tree.

Loving every moment of the spotlight, Amber oohed and aahed over each gift. Johanna found herself wishing Amber could open presents for her on her birthday, as Johanna always wanted to find somewhere to hide when people watched her.

Once Amber had opened the last present, her mother produced a small package from behind her back. "You have one last gift, Amber."

Amber's eyes lit with delight as their little sister, Bethany, urged her to open it quickly. Relishing her last present, Amber gingerly tore back the paper. She opened the box and pulled out the single sheet of folded-up paper. She scrunched her nose. "What is this?"

Her dad smiled. "Well, open it."

Johanna feared she would burst, she was so excited for Amber to figure out what it was. She rubbed her hands together while Amber unfolded the paper and read the top. Her sister's eyes widened and her mouth fell open. Amber jumped up from her chair and waved the paper in the air. "Is this what I think it is?"

Johanna burst into laughter.

"Is it?" Amber looked at her parents again.

Her dad stood and wrapped his arms around Amber. "It's your enrollment paper for high school. You're going to be a high school senior this year."

Amber squealed and wrapped her arms around her dad. Her mother joined the hug, and Johanna could wait no longer. She grabbed Bethany and the two of them wrapped their arms around their parents and Amber.

Her father broke away. "Remember you're to be a light in the world. If we feel this is too much, we will take you back out of school."

"I know, Daddy."

He patted Amber's back as he addressed their friends from church. "Why don't we all go inside so Amber can play the piece she's been working on? My girl here is planning to play in college."

Johanna grabbed hold of Amber's arm. "I'm so happy for you."

"Did you know?"

Johanna nodded. "I thought I would pop if your birthday didn't hurry up and get here."

They walked inside and Amber sat at the piano. The room was crowded, but most of the younger children stayed outside playing games.

Amber beamed when she began to play. Her fingers moved over the keys with a grace and ease Johanna had never seen from anyone else. Happiness filled her for the pure joy that shone from her sister's face.

Johanna looked around the room. She spied Gavin watching Amber. There was something about the way he looked at her. It reminded her of the way her daddy looked at her mama.

Again, she wondered if she should feel some sort of jealousy. She didn't, and no matter what her mother had experienced, Johanna could never be the one to take that look of affection away from her sister.

seven

A few days after Drew and Melody returned from their honeymoon, Mike walked up the sidewalk to Nick and Addy's house. They'd planned a get-together with Wyatt and Gracie, Drew and Melody, Nick and Addy, and Mike. He felt like a complete fifth wheel; actually, it was more like a seventh wheel.

Before he reached the porch steps, the front door swung open and Addy ran out. She beamed at Mike. "Gracie's water broke."

Mike lifted his eyebrows and glanced back at the driveway. He hadn't noticed Wyatt's car.

"They hadn't made it here yet." Addy turned back toward the house. "Come on, Melody. Just leave the water boiling. The men can finish the corn on the cob."

"I'm coming." Melody's voice sounded from inside the door.

Addy turned back toward Mike. "It's just going to be you, Nick, and Drew. We're heading to the hospital. There's plenty of food. You all can just hang out here. . . ."

"I'm ready." Melody raced through the front door. Drew followed close behind her. She started down the steps when Drew pulled her back and kissed her lips.

Mike's cheeks warmed at the display of affection. Not because he was embarrassed, but because he realized how much he wanted that.

Melody pushed Drew away. "Honey, I've got to go. Gracie

waited for us to get home. I can't ask her to wait for me to get to the hospital, too."

Drew laughed. "Melody, I don't think you had all that much say in when that woman went into labor."

Melody swatted the air with her hand. She glanced at Mike and waved. "Nice to see you again, Mike."

He nodded and then moved out of her and Addy's way as they barreled down the steps. Within seconds, the two had jumped into Addy's car and were headed down the road.

Drew opened the door wide and motioned to Mike. "Looks like it's just going to be the three of us."

Mike grinned. He was glad. It had been a long time since he'd spent time with just his buddies. Except for Wyatt's bachelor party and then Nick's bachelor party and then Drew's. But even then poor Drew had been so torn up and excited about the upcoming wedding that they weren't able to enjoy the truck pull they'd gone to.

He wondered if he'd ever have a bachelor party they could go to.

He walked inside as Nick was coming in the back door holding a plate of freshly grilled burgers. Nick bellowed, "Looks like we can eat as much as we want."

Mike surveyed the counter filled with hamburgers and fixings, homemade potato salad and coleslaw, corn on the cob cooking in a pot on the stove, and some kind of cobbler, probably blackberry, sitting on the kitchen table. The variety and volume of food had certainly improved with the additions of his friends' wives. It looked delicious, and his stomach rumbled in response.

Drew patted his back. "I think the man wants to eat."

Mike turned and grabbed Drew's hand in a firm handshake. "It's good to see you, buddy. Sounded like you were having a good time on your honeymoon."

Drew's eyes lit up and he beamed brighter than the sun beats down on a man in the middle of a field on the hottest day of August. "It was awesome. So did you take my advice before your date with Lacy?"

Nick stopped loading his plate with food and turned toward Drew and Mike. "Wait a minute. Are you saying you talked to Mike before he went on his date? Weren't you on your honeymoon?"

Mike laughed. "Yes, he was. I couldn't believe it when I saw his number on my phone."

Drew shrugged and grabbed an empty plate. "Mike's my friend and I wanted him to relax and enjoy his date."

Nick snickered. "He's my friend, too, but he's the last thing I'd be thinking about on my honeymoon."

Drew put down the plate and lifted his hands in surrender. "Okay. Okay. I get it." He placed a hamburger bun on the plate. "So, how did the date go?"

Mike growled. "It was awful."

"What happened?" asked Nick as he turned off the stove then jabbed a corncob with his fork.

Mike plopped an oversize spoonful of potato salad on his plate. "We weren't very compatible. I don't believe we have the same beliefs when it comes to our faith. She just— I really don't want to say anything negative. Let's just leave it with we didn't agree on a few things."

"Yeah. I was afraid of that." Drew took a bite of his hamburger then headed toward the kitchen table and sat down.

With their plates overflowing, Nick and Mike joined Drew at the table.

"That's too bad, man." Nick took a drink of his soft drink.

"I spent too long worrying over that girl." Mike swallowed a bite of coleslaw. "Now I've already got another gal floating around in my mind all the time. Course, I should be afraid of her. Every time I see her she hits me in some way."

"What?" Drew leaned closer to the table and shook a pickle at him. "Mike McCauley, the man who warded off women all through middle and high school, who had a crush on the same woman for three years, goes out with her, and finds out he doesn't like her, so he finds another girl he's interested in—in a week's time?"

Mike wrinkled his nose and gawked at Drew. "Man, I have no idea what you just said."

Nick swallowed a big bite of hamburger then laughed. "So there's a new girl. Tell us about her."

Mike told them about Johanna knocking the bottles of bubbles out of his hands and then busting his lip at the barn before the wedding. Then he shared how she'd run him off the sidewalk and then slammed into his ankles in the grocery store. He held up his leg and lifted the back of his jeans to show them the mark. "I'm telling you the woman practically ran me over with that cart."

"Hmm, a cute woman who beats up on you every time you see her." Drew shrugged. "I guess she sounds interesting, if you like to be covered in bumps and bruises."

Nick guffawed and punched Drew in the arm. "Maybe you should go for her."

Drew winced and rubbed the spot Nick punched. "Ow. That

hurt. I'm still a little burned there from the honeymoon. It's above my farmer's tan line."

Mike almost spit out his food at Drew's whining. He turned to Nick. "Actually, I've been kind of thinking that myself, but I don't know how to get in touch with her. I know what she looks like and I know her name, but that's all I know."

"So who is she?" Drew asked.

"She's a cutie, long blond hair. All I know is her name is Johanna Smith. We introduced ourselves at the store in case the next time she ran into me I'd need to go to the hospital."

Nick pulled the hamburger out of his mouth without taking a bite. "Did you say Johanna Smith?"

"Yeah."

Nick placed his hamburger back on the plate and touched his arm about midway down. "Long blond hair. Thin girl. Maybe a little shorter than Addy."

Mike nodded.

Nick smacked the table. "Doesn't that just beat all. Addy and I just worked with that gal last week at the library."

"What?"

"Yeah. Remember I told you the librarian lady had asked me to do this fair thing for the preschool and kindergarten kids and bring one of my calves for the kiddos to look at?"

Mike nodded. He had a vague remembrance of Nick telling him something about that.

Nick pointed his fork at Mike. "That girl. Johanna Smith. She was one of the librarian's helpers there. She read a book about spring to the kids." He shoved a bite of coleslaw in his mouth. "Seemed like a nice girl," he muttered. "Addy really liked her."

"The library, huh?" Mike sat back in his chair. It made sense. The library was just a ways down the road from where she'd run into him on the sidewalk. He'd have to conjure up a reason to patron the place. After several moments, he looked up at his friends who were both staring at him and grinning. Warmth flooded his face and he swatted at them. "Let's talk about something else. Drew, tell us about Florida."

Drew shared that Melody had talked him into going scuba diving. He raved about the various fish, stingrays, and jellyfish he'd had the opportunity to see.

Mike tried to focus on his friend, but his mind kept drifting to when he'd have an opportunity to head to the library. He could say he needed to do some research on their computers, but that would be a lie, as he had Internet availability at his home. Though he enjoyed magazines, he wasn't much of a book reader. Informational books maybe, but he did most of his reading off his computer.

I could just go in there and tell her I'd like to go on a date, rather than wait three years like I did with Lacy.

The very idea made his heart race and his hands grow clammy. If she said no, he'd be mortified. *I'm still going to be embarrassed even if she says yes.*

Drew's voice interrupted his thoughts. "And then we jumped into a pool of sharks, and one of them bit off Melody's leg."

Mike wrinkled his nose and furrowed his eyebrows. "What?"

Drew laughed. "Are you still with us, buddy? I think you went off into space for a while."

Mike squinted at his friend. "Aren't you just hilarious?"

Nick elbowed Drew's side. "I think our friend here is pining over another girl."

Mike didn't admit it aloud, but he believed he was.

⠀⠀⠀⠀⠀⠀⠀⠀⠀⠀⠀⠀⠀⠀⠀⠀⠀⠀⠀⠀⠀⠀⠀⠀⠀⠀⠀⠀⠀⠀⠀⠀⠀ ❧

"It's opening day for frog gigging!" Johanna exclaimed when she walked in the house after work. "I've got the gigs all ready."

Johanna and her mother had a tradition to frog gig up at their family's pond on opening night. She looked forward to the May event every year. The day before, Johanna would search the shed for their gigs, which were simply metal three-pronged forks attached to old broomsticks—homemade fishing spears. Near midnight, wearing the oldest pants and shoes they could find, she and her mother would walk and steal around the banks of the pond with a bright flashlight in one hand and the gig in the other.

Listening carefully for the distinct *varuump* of a bullfrog, they would shine the light in its eyes, freezing the amphibian for a moment, then jab the gig into the frog's body, and stick it in an onion sack. After collecting several, they'd head home, clean their catch, and the next day the family would enjoy a dinner of fried frog legs. As long as their dad didn't get anxious and make their mom fry them up with breakfast.

"Johanna." Her mother's voice sounded weak as she called from her upstairs bedroom.

"Mama doesn't feel well." Bethany walked into the kitchen. "She asked me to start dinner. Amber's in the basement doing laundry."

Johanna made her way up the stairs and into her parents' bedroom. Her mother's face was as pale as the white sheets, and droplets of sweat beaded on her forehead. She tried to smile. "I don't think I can make it gigging tonight. I believe I've caught a bug."

Johanna picked up a washrag from the end table and wiped off her mother's brow. "I believe you have." She looked at her mother's nearly empty glass. "You want me to get you some water?"

Her mother nodded. "Haven't held much down today, but I wouldn't mind to try a few saltine crackers again. The Mitchell boys started getting sick from a stomach bug right after they left the other night. I'd say I caught it from one of them."

Johanna nodded. "I'll go get you some water and crackers."

She made her way down the stairs to the main floor as Amber clunked up from the basement with a load of folded clothes. She placed the basket on the table with a huff. "Whew. Those are heavy." She turned toward Johanna. "I told Mama I'd go gigging with you tonight."

Johanna lifted her eyebrows and pointed to her sister. "You're going to go gigging with me tonight." To her knowledge, her sister had never touched a live frog let alone a dead one, though she never minded to eat her fill of Johanna and their mother's catch.

Amber giggled as she smacked and rubbed her hands together. "I know. There's a first time for everything."

Bethany wrinkled her nose and flipped a mass of long blond hair over her shoulder. "I wouldn't mind to pick up the frogs, but I don't want to kill them."

"Don't play with your hair while you're cooking," Johanna reprimanded her youngest sister.

Bethany stuck out her tongue. "Good thing you're not my boss." She stuck out her bottom lip. "You could have asked me nicely."

Johanna wrapped one arm around Bethany, who had always

been the most sensitive of the three girls. "You're right. I just hate that Mama's sick. She loves gigging. Do you want to go with Amber and me tonight?"

Bethany turned back to the hamburger frying in the skillet. "No way."

Johanna looked back at Amber. "I think you're going to have a lot more fun than you expect."

She took a can of chicken noodle soup from the pantry and opened it. She poured its contents in a pan and added a cup of water. Her mother had only asked for crackers and water, but she looked so pale that maybe she could try a bit of soup, too.

Once it finished warming, she gathered the soup, saltines, and water for her mother and went back upstairs. Her mom had already propped several pillows up behind her. Johanna smiled at her mom. "I hear Amber's going with me tonight."

Her mom braved a weak chuckle. "You'll have to let me know how it goes. Hopefully, I'll feel better by tomorrow so I can enjoy your catch." Her mother frowned. "Although the thought of it right now makes my stomach turn all over again."

Johanna placed the bowl of soup on the end table. "Then don't think about that right now. Think about holding down some soup and then resting some more. The girls and I can handle the house tonight."

"I know you can. The three of you have been such a blessing."

Her mother took a few sips of water and ate a couple of spoonfuls of the soup. Johanna could tell Mama already felt fatigued again. She walked out of the room and downstairs to help her sisters.

With dinner finished and the dishes done, her father retired to his bedroom to read where he could watch over their mother, and her sisters settled into the family room to watch some evening television.

Johanna nestled down on the couch in the living area to enjoy the latest release of her favorite fishing magazine. John James wrote about his first experience frog gigging with his little brother. As the article went on, the emotion he felt toward his younger sibling became more apparent. At the close, he talked about how his brother had passed away unexpectedly.

A lone tear slipped down Johanna's cheek. She couldn't imagine, didn't even want to think about, what it would be like to lose one of her sisters. John James had such a sensitive, caring spirit, and he was able to express it with his words. Again, she yearned to meet the man one day. She didn't get all excited about autographs and pictures, but she'd still like to be able to put a face with the stories she read.

She glanced at the grandfather clock that had been in her father's family for five generations. It was ten o'clock according to the old antique. She looked at her watch to confirm it told the correct time, as it only did half the time. It did.

Anticipation swelled in her belly as she stood and made her way into the family room. Bethany had just stood up and turned off the television. Johanna noted Amber sitting on the couch, a mixed look of fatigue and dread etched her face. Bethany patted Amber's knee. "Have fun with Johanna, sis."

Johanna giggled. She hooked her arm around Amber's and helped her sister to her feet. "It's really not that bad. You liked to play in the mud when we were kids. It's just like that all over again."

Amber wrinkled her nose. "I haven't purposely played in the mud in *many* years, and I *never* recall stabbing innocent creatures when I did."

Johanna laughed out loud. "I need someone else to help me slay the bullfrogs, or I wouldn't ask you to go." She elbowed her sister's side. "I promise it will be fun."

Amber slumped away from the couch and meandered up the stairs. By the time Johanna was finally able to get her sister on her way to change into old clothes and shoes and had changed into her own grubbies, it was almost eleven o'clock. They made their way downstairs and grabbed an onion sack, two flashlights, and the fishgigs.

"I can't believe I'm doing this," Amber moaned.

Johanna hooked her arm around Amber's. "Just think of all those yummy fried frog legs we'll eat tomorrow evening."

Amber whined. "I don't think that helps."

Feeling mischievous, she winked at her sister. "We'll have to be sure to cut the tendons in their legs correctly so they don't hop out of the skillet while they're frying. Remember that one time—"

Amber wrapped one hand around her stomach. "I think I'm going to be sick."

Johanna giggled. "You know I'm just teasing you. I know how to cut the tendons."

Amber moaned, and Johanna burst into laughter.

They walked up to the pond, and Johanna sucked in her breath at the beauty of the moon shining down on the pond. "God's amazing, isn't He?"

Amber looked around. "It is pretty up here. I can see why you like to come up here so much."

Words couldn't adequately express how Johanna felt each time she walked up to the family's pond. For so many years she had been basking in her Savior from this spot. It was like nostalgia mixed with repentance intertwined with worship. She couldn't count the times she'd sat on the bench and felt as if God wrapped His mammoth arms around her in strength, forgiveness, and comfort.

"I do love this spot." She looked back at her sister. "But let's get to work. You need to listen for the bullfrog then shine the light in his eyes. If you're too nervous to gig him, motion for me and I'll do it."

Amber nodded.

Within moments, they'd found and speared two bullfrogs. As they walked the bank of the pond, slipping every once in a while into its waters, Johanna found it increasingly difficult to keep from laughing outright. Her sister became more enthusiastic than Johanna would have imagined though she wouldn't actually kill the frog. The goofy faces Amber made sent Johanna into giggles, and she missed some that she could have gotten.

By the time they had expended their energy, the girls had collected ten frogs. More than enough for their meal the next day. Giddy and giggling, they made their way to the back door, pulled off their sopping shoes, and stripped off their pants and jackets until they stood in the shorts and T-shirts they'd worn underneath. They cleaned their catch in the sink in the mudroom to avoid making a mess in the kitchen.

Amber brushed a stray strand of hair out from her eyes with the back of her hand. "That was a lot of fun. Now I know why you and Mama look forward to it so much."

"I told ya you'd like it."

"At the party, Gavin was talking about how much fun it is.

I told him he was crazy, but he insisted I should go." Her sister's face flushed. "Even if he had to take me himself."

Johanna bit her bottom lip as she studied her sister. She looked back at the frogs and continued to clean them. "He seemed to enjoy your piano playing."

Amber's voice raised a pitch. "I know."

Johanna flipped the water off her hands, wiped them on a towel, and turned to her sister. "Amber, do you *like* Gavin?"

Amber huffed. "Of course not." She shifted her weight from one foot to the other. "I mean, he's too old for me."

"Only four years, and just barely that."

"Yeah, but I'm only seventeen."

Johanna leaned against the wall and studied her sister's expression. "Next year, four years won't be too much."

"But—"

Johanna crossed her arms in front of her chest. "Just so you know, I don't like him that way."

Amber looked at Johanna. "You don't?"

Johanna shook her head.

"But Mama always acts like—"

"I told Mama I don't like him that way." She moved closer to her sister. "But you know what, I think he likes you, too."

"You do?"

Johanna nodded. "But you would need to wait a year."

Amber giggled. "I know. Besides, I want to go to college. I'm not worried about a guy right now." She looked at Johanna, ducked her chin, and smiled. "Not really anyway."

Johanna grabbed her sister in a big hug. "Let's finish these frogs up. We all have plenty to do tomorrow."

eight

Exhaustion oozed from every one of Johanna's 206 bones. It had been two weeks since she and Amber went frog gigging the first time. Since then Amber had her out at the pond and at the stream, which was a good twenty-minute trek from the house, nearly every other night. Last night, she hadn't slipped into bed until well past two o'clock.

Rubbing her eyes with the back of her hand, she peered up at the top shelf of books. She'd been shelf reading—making sure all the books had been put back in correct alphabetical order—for the past two hours. The names and titles were beginning to blur, and Johanna knew she needed to take a break. But her lunch wasn't for an hour, and she really didn't have a good excuse, except that she'd been staying up too late frog gigging.

Noting that several books sat beneath the return slot, she decided to switch tasks and check them in while her eyes rested a moment. She made her way to the front desk, smiling at a young girl sprawled out on her belly in the children's section, trying to sound out the words of a picture book.

Memories of doing the same thing while perched on her mother's lap filled her with joy. The only thing that could bring her more joy would be to have a child of her own to help sound out words, to teach, to lose herself in the words of a story.

She walked behind the counter and sat on the stool. After

picking up the books, she logged into the computer and started checking them in.

She felt someone standing in front of the desk before the person actually said anything. "Can I help you?" She smiled as she looked up then sucked in her breath when she saw Mike standing there. Taken aback, she lost her balance on the swivel chair and fell off the side. Mike reached across the desk to help her, but she held tight to the lip of the wooden desk, praying her feet wouldn't give way.

He drew back his hand, and the amused smile she'd noted he often wore around her surfaced again. She swallowed. "Hello, Mike."

She continued to grip the side of the desk until she feared she'd rip the wood in two. In an attempt to be inconspicuous and to try to gain control of her composure, she drew in a slow inward breath. Finally letting go of the wood, she swiped a strand of hair behind her ear. "Is there anything I can help you with?"

The expression on his face changed, and Johanna noted a deep-red wave trailing up his neck. For once, he looked nervous. Wanting to put him at ease, Johanna's anxiety dimmed and she smiled fully at him. She leaned forward. "I'll try not to hurt you this time."

She must have said the right thing, because Mike laughed and the tension in his expression subsided. "I'm not worried that you'll hurt me."

He cleared his throat, and Johanna waited for him to continue. He started to open his mouth, but he averted his gaze to the fishing magazine she'd brought back to the library that morning. He pointed to it. "You read that?"

Johanna bit her bottom lip and nodded. "I'm an avid outdoorswoman." She pressed her fingers under her eyes. "I've been out late frog gigging way too much lately. You can tell by the bags under my eyes."

Johanna's stomach turned. She'd said more to him in the last few minutes than she normally said to Mrs. Love in a full day's work.

He raised his eyebrows as if surprised by her admission. He pointed at the magazine again. "It's a good magazine. From Kentucky, I believe."

Johanna nodded. "Yes, but it's gained a nationwide following."

"Has it?"

"Yes." She picked it up and opened to the article written by John James. "This author specifically writes as if he's from around here. His last article was about frog gigging with his brother." She let out a deep sigh. "But his brother passed away unexpectedly. I could tell by the way he wrote it devastated him."

"Really?"

Johanna noticed Mike looked away from her for a moment, but she continued. "I'd like to meet him. I've got him pictured in my mind as a bushy-bearded, gray-haired grandpa type with—" She looked up at Mike and noted the amused smile had returned. Embarrassed, she put the magazine back on the desk and clasped her hands. *I cannot believe I am talking this man's ear off. God, what is going on with me?*

Mike nodded. "You can go on."

Johanna shook her head and feared her embarrassment was going to turn her stomach to the point that it made its way up her throat. He really wouldn't know what to think if she upchucked all over him.

She swallowed again. "Is there anything I can help you with?"

"Actually there is." Mike cleared his throat once more and shifted his weight. "I was wondering."

She glanced at his hands and noted his fingers crumpling the ball cap he must have been wearing before he'd come into the library.

He continued. "I was wondering if you'd let me take you for a soft drink when you get off work."

He blew out a quick breath, and for an instant Johanna wondered at how hard it had been for him to say those words. But what he said didn't seem to register in her mind. She stared at him for a moment, trying to put together his request. No one had asked her on a date before. No one.

Which made sense, because her family didn't believe in dating in the world's sense. They believed more in friendship that moved to a dating of sorts with the intent to marry.

She must have stared at him too long because he took a step back. "It's okay if you're busy."

She peered into the blue-green eyes of the man she'd thought so much about though knew so little about. She was attracted to him as she had never been attracted to a man before, and everything in her wanted to say yes.

Then say yes, her spirit prodded.

Warmth flooded her cheeks, but she nodded. "Okay."

Mike stepped forward again; his eyebrows rose in surprise. "Really? I thought you were going to say no. What time do you get off work?"

"Five."

"Okay." He backed away from the desk and lifted his hand

in a wave. "Well, I'll see you then."

"Okay." Still in a daze, Johanna watched him leave the building. She jolted back to the present when one of the books she'd been checking in fell to the ground.

Spotting one of the aides, she raced over to her and told her she needed a quick break. She couldn't believe she'd agreed. She had to call Mama.

❧

Excitement filled him as he walked out of the library. *So she fixes homemade chocolate crème pie, helps people in need, likes the outdoors, and loves John James's articles. God, where has this woman been all my life?*

He made his way to the diner. He hadn't eaten there since his and Lacy's date several weeks ago, but the guys had talked Wyatt into having lunch with them. The poor man looked like the walking dead after working all day and helping Gracie take care of his toddling boy, Wyatt Jr., and their new daughter, Greta.

Excitement switched to dread as he walked through the front door of the diner. Maybe he didn't have anything to worry about. She could be off today, and they wouldn't have to see each other. He scanned the room, spotted his friends, and walked toward them. He didn't see Lacy anywhere.

With a sigh of relief, he sat down next to Wyatt and patted his friend on the back. "How's it going, man?"

The man looked like he hadn't slept in weeks. Fine lines strayed from red-rimmed eyes. His color looked as splotchy as Gracie's had when he saw her just before she had the baby. Wyatt muttered, "I'm living. Barely."

Nick guffawed from across the table. "You said you wanted a bus full of kids."

Wyatt looked up at him and scowled. "I don't believe I said that."

Drew chimed in. "Oh, yes you did."

Wyatt rubbed his hand across his stubble-covered jaw. "Somebody should have shot me when I said that."

They all laughed, including Wyatt. "Nah." He turned his coffee cup right side up as a sign to the waitress to fill it up. Mike imagined Wyatt had been drinking a lot of java lately. "These days are just a bit harder on the body. She'll get into a sleeping routine soon enough."

Mike looked at Nick. "So, how's Addy doing?"

Nick nodded. "Doing well. Still having some sickness, but we go back to the doctor in two weeks."

Mike turned toward Drew. "What about you? You and Melody having kids yet?" He pointed to the other two guys. "You don't want them to outdo you, now do you?"

Drew lifted both hands in the air. "I'll surrender on that one. Be the loser for sure. I'm not ready to give up alone time with Melody yet." He winked then he nudged Mike with his elbow. "But what about you? Did you ask the librarian out on a date yet?"

Before Mike could answer, a familiar female voice sounded above them. "I'll take your order, boys." She smirked at Mike, and he knew she'd heard what Drew said. "Mike, I assume you'll try something different today."

Mike looked down at the menu. *I guess she's working today after all.* He glanced across the table. His friends were studying their menus as well. He handed Lacy the menu. "Nope. I want the same. Meat loaf and mashed potatoes."

She took his friends' orders then stomped away from the table.

Nick leaned across the table. "What did you do to make her so mad?"

Mike shook his head and shrugged. "It wasn't a good date. I told you we disagreed on some things."

Drew punched his arm. "Geez, man. I hope she doesn't take it out on our food."

Mike didn't respond to the comment. Instead, he looked at Drew and said, "To answer your earlier question, yes, I'm taking the librarian for a soft drink tonight."

Wyatt howled. "Good job, man. Two dates in one month. You're finally coming out of your shell."

Lacy walked out from the kitchen with their soft drinks on a tray.

Mike stared pointedly at his friends and whispered, "We probably shouldn't talk about it right now."

She placed their drinks in front of each of them. "Your orders will be out in a minute."

Mike looked up at her. "Thanks, Lacy."

She glared at him and walked away. He didn't want her to be angry with him, but he felt certain that the true Lacy showed up for their date. And he didn't want to date a woman who behaved that way. Mike smiled at his friends. "Let's talk about something else."

Wyatt pulled out his phone and passed it around for them to see the latest snapshots of Wyatt and Greta. This prompted Nick to show off Addy's ultrasound picture that they'd all seen at least five times. When Drew pulled out his phone to show off the beach photos from his honeymoon, Mike feared he was going to be sick. Thankfully, Lacy arrived with their food, and they started to eat.

They had a good visit, and Mike was glad they'd been able to hang out for a while. So much had changed in the last few years. He remembered the bet they'd made to ward off women. In truth, he'd enjoyed those years. They hunted and fished whenever they wanted. Had tractor and truck pulls. Just pretty much did whatever they wanted whenever they wanted.

All that had changed for Wyatt, Nick, and Drew. Now they made late evening trips to the grocery store for items they'd never even known existed until they'd gotten hitched. They couldn't hang out on a whim or rush to a tractor pull without some kind of prior planning.

But Mike had never seen them so happy.

He paid his bill and left the tip for Lacy. He wanted an opportunity to talk to her again, but he didn't know what he would say. He couldn't take back that he thought she'd been wrong for the way she acted on their date, but he didn't want to be cruel to her, either.

She seemed to avoid coming out from the kitchen, so Mike walked on out of the diner. He said good-bye to his friends and they each went their separate ways. Mike headed back to his truck. He had four hours until he needed to be back for Johanna. He had plenty to do on the farm. Hopefully, he'd keep his hands busy enough to keep his mind off five o'clock.

nine

Johanna wasn't surprised when her father pulled up in front of the library during her lunch break. She knew her mother would hunt him down, wherever he happened to be doing handyman work for the day. He walked through the door, holding up his lunch bag. "Mind if I eat with you today?"

Johanna smiled. She knew most of the girls she worked with would be upset if their fathers wanted to know every time a guy asked them for a soft drink. But Johanna was different. She felt protected and loved that her daddy would leave his work, find her, and give her advice about the man she was meeting.

She pointed out the window to a bench beside a flower bed and fountain. "I'll meet you there. I take my break in five minutes."

"Sounds good."

She watched as her father tipped his head at an older gentleman who sat at a table perusing a magazine. He settled onto the bench but didn't take out any of his food. She knew he would wait to say grace with her. Turning back to her work, she placed another DVD in its spot.

Mrs. Love approached her. "Go ahead and take your lunch five minutes early." She smiled. "No need in making your father wait to eat."

"Thanks, Mrs. Love." Johanna went into the break area, took her lunch from the refrigerator, then joined her father on the bench.

"I'm supposing Mama called you."

He nodded and took her hand. "Let's say grace first."

Johanna bowed her head and listened to her father's genuine petition for blessing over their food and their time together. She may have felt snippets of rebellion against her parents during her early teen years, but at twenty-one, her father had proven to her time and again that he sought God's will and her best interest. Though she was attracted to Mike, she'd accept his wisdom and love and heed whatever he said.

He bit into his ham and cheese sandwich and swallowed it down with a chug of water. Johanna took a small bite of hers, as well, knowing he'd share his thoughts any moment.

"Your mama tells me a young man asked to take you to get a soft drink after work today."

Johanna nodded. "He did."

"And you accepted."

She nodded again.

"Do you know anything about this man?"

Hesitation and a sense of foolishness nibbled at her gut. She averted his gaze. "I really only know his name is Mike McCauley." Dread began to sink into her gut. "I guess I don't."

He cupped her chin with his finger, forcing her to look at his eyes. "Then why would you say yes?"

Her cheeks blazed, and she felt the foolishness of her acceptance. How could she explain to her father that she'd simply had a feeling that he was a nice man? Didn't she know that scripture told her the heart was "deceitful above all things" and that Christians were to be "shrewd as snakes and as innocent as doves"? *God, I should have talked with my parents first.*

"Johanna, I can tell you feel foolish for having accepted his offer. You should never accept a date, so to speak, from a man you do not know."

She nodded. Her father was right. "I'll tell him when he comes at five."

She looked at her father and noticed a grin forming on his lips. "Now, I didn't say that." He stuck a chip in his mouth, chewed, and swallowed. "You know your mother thinks Gavin Mitchell would be a good match for you."

Johanna sighed. "Yes, I know."

"But I have a feeling Gavin has his sights on another girl. Another Smith girl, possibly?"

Johanna couldn't hold back sharing her smile. "I believe you're right again."

She felt it nearly impossible that her father would pick up on Gavin's and Amber's interest in one another. Her mother, who was always in tune with everything happening with her daughters, hadn't even realized it.

"Which brings us back to Mike McCauley."

"Daddy, I said I'd tell him when he gets here. You're right—"

Her father held up his hand. "I happen to know who the young man is. And I know his father."

Johanna perked up. "You do? Is he a good man? I have a feeling"—she pointed to her stomach—"down deep in my gut that he's a Christian, and that he—"

Her cheeks warmed again as her father grinned at her excitement. He grabbed her hand with his left hand and patted the top of it with his right. "As a matter of fact I believe he is a good man. A good Christian man. And you have my blessing to have a soft drink with him tonight."

Johanna leaned closer to her father. "Tell me what you know about him. Where does he work? Where does he go to church?"

Her father placed the remaining contents of his lunch back in the bag and stood. "All of those things you need to find out on your own when you talk with him tonight. Your mother and I will be praying for you. You know we feel dating in the traditional sense leads to unnecessary heartache."

He patted the top of her head as he used to do when she was a girl. "But you have to get to know a man to know if he's the one God has planned for you." He kissed her head. "See you later, sweetie."

She watched as he walked back to his truck and drove away. Glancing down at her lunch, she realized she'd hardly eaten anything at all. Though her stomach churned too much to eat all she'd brought, she forced a little down so she wouldn't be hungry the rest of the day.

Her father's words played and replayed in her mind. A good Christian man. She longed for a good Christian man. Closing her eyes, she lifted her face to the sky. *I'm so attracted to Mike, and to learn he is a Christian. . .* She sucked in her breath. *You know my greatest desire is to love and serve You, and You also know I want a husband and a family. It's what I've longed for since I was a little girl.*

She tried to rein in her feelings. Her prayer sounded too dramatic to her own mind. She didn't know this man, and she was practically planning their marriage. Not even the wedding, but their life together. *Jesus, I've never felt this way about anyone. I don't want to simply follow my heart. I want to follow Your will. Show me tonight if Mike McCauley is the man You have for me.*

Mike sat across from Johanna at the Main Street Café. He knew her to be attractive from the brief encounters they'd had, but now he saw how truly beautiful she was. He could tell she was nervous, and she seemed even shyer than Mike, but he still snuck peeks of her. When she smiled, she had the slightest dimple in her left cheek. And her teeth were perfectly straight and white. Her skin didn't have a blemish, not even a freckle that he could find. She was so naturally gorgeous he had a hard time not staring at her.

Trying to start some kind of conversation, he asked, "How was work today?"

She glanced at him for a moment and smiled. "It was good. Thank you."

She twisted the tissue in her hands until he thought the poor thing would crumble to shreds on the table. She cleared her throat. "So, what do you do for a living, Mike?"

"Mostly, I farm with my dad."

She nodded and averted her gaze back to the tissue.

The waitress arrived. She pushed the blue cap she wore off her forehead. "My name's Zelda." She pointed to the name tag on her button-down uniform shirt and winked at Mike. "I'll be helping you this evening." She pulled a notepad and pen from the apron around her waist, and Mike noticed she wore several rings on each finger. She looked at Johanna. "What can I get you, honey?"

"Well. . ." Johanna's voice came out barely above a whisper.

"Honey, you're going to have to talk louder than that." Zelda pointed the pen to her ear.

Johanna sat up and spoke a little louder. "A chocolate shake with whipped—"

"Sweetie." Zelda shook her head at Johanna. "I've been doing this a long time." She pointed to the graying hair sticking from behind her cap. "I don't have much hearing left in me. You're going to have to—"

Mike spoke up. "We'd like two chocolate shakes with whipped cream on top."

Johanna smiled at him, melting his heart.

Zelda nodded. "Would you like cherries, too?"

Johanna nodded, and Mike said they would.

Zelda grabbed their menus and tapped the side of them on the top of the table. "I'll get them right out."

The café was busy with the dinner crowd coming in. Mike wished he'd asked her if she'd like to eat dinner. He hadn't thought of it when he went to the library, because he thought she might get off earlier. He assumed she was probably hungry by now, but she was so quiet and bashful that he didn't want to ask.

Unsure what to say, he took in the fifties memorabilia around the café. The checkerboard patterned walls had vinyl records hanging on them. In the back stood an old-fashioned jukebox that played real records. Johanna had picked the perfect drink, as their chocolate shakes were the best he'd ever tasted, made from scratch.

He glanced back at Johanna. This wasn't going as he planned. He figured she'd be shy. He couldn't be upset with her for it. He tended to be bashful as well. But they had to be able to talk about something.

A family walked in the door. The little girl must have recognized Johanna, because her face lit up and she raced to their table. "Hi, Miss Johanna, do you remember me?"

Johanna beamed and she wrapped the child in a hug. "Of course I remember you, Marly. How is first grade?"

The little girl shared about a boy who enjoyed picking on her, about the slide that had a nail popped up on the ladder that cut her foot, about the toilets that terrified her because they flushed by themselves. When her parents finally motioned for her to rejoin them, she hugged Johanna once more. Johanna whispered, "I'm glad you're enjoying it."

The little girl giggled and skipped to her parents. Johanna laughed. She looked at Mike. "Marly is so full of life." She leaned over and placed her hand beside her mouth to whisper. "She's just a little dramatic." She sat back and shrugged. "But you can't help but love her."

The child had broken the tension, and just as Mike expected he realized Johanna was a breath of fresh air. Her genuineness shined through. Mike asked about her family, and she shared how much she cared for and respected her parents and two younger sisters.

By the time they started talking about his family their shakes had arrived, and they laughed as they tried to get the thick shake up through the straw. Giving up, they both ate their shakes with a spoon.

He wiped his mouth with a napkin. "So tell me about this avid outdoorswoman stuff."

She spread her arms open. "I love God's creation. I love hunting and fishing and frog gigging and camping and hiking. I have a special place at my house where I fellowship with God every day."

"So, you're a Christian?" He nodded. "I had a feeling you were."

She leaned forward. "I had a feeling you were also."

"I am."

"I know. My dad found out." She covered her mouth with her hand.

"Checking up on me, were you?"

"I had to make sure you weren't trying to seek your own revenge for the many times I've attacked you."

Mike twirled the spoon in his glass then ate his last bite of shake. "You've definitely been trying to get my attention."

Johanna waved her hands. She reached across the table and grabbed his arm. "I promise I wasn't."

Realizing what she'd done, she pulled her hand away, and Mike missed the feel of her hand on his skin. He gazed down at his arm and noticed the time. He looked up at her just as Zelda passed their table with another armload of fresh burger baskets. "Johanna, it's after 6:30. Let me buy you a hamburger. You've got to be as hungry as I am. Those burgers smell delicious."

Johanna glanced toward Zelda then up at the *Happy Days* clock on the wall behind her. "They sure do. I think I'll take you up on that offer." She bit her bottom lip. "I'm going to run outside and call my parents so they won't be worried."

Mike nodded and motioned for Zelda while Johanna stepped outside. He could see her through the window talking to either her mother or father. She seemed every bit as pleased with their date as he was. *God, thanks for having her bump into me. Sorry it took three times.*

ten

Johanna couldn't sleep that night. She'd had a wonderful time with Mike at the café. Even better than she'd prayed for. She forced herself to wait until as close to daybreak as she could stand before she slipped into some clothes and grabbed her tote bag. She patted her leg for Max then headed out the back door and up to the pond.

It would be thirty minutes or more before the sunrise. She sat on the bench and basked in the cool breeze kissing her cheeks and the moonlight bouncing off the still waters. Lifting her face to the heavens, she prayed to her Master and King. *Lord, he's just what I've dreamed of. He loves You, Jesus. And he's easy to talk to. He's a farmer, God. I could continue to bask in Your land. And he's handsome.*

She stood, opened her arms, and twirled around. Closing her eyes, she reveled in the contentment of glorifying the Father and praised Him that it appeared He would give her the desires of her heart.

"Did your family tell you I stopped by your house last night?"

With a gasp, Johanna stopped spinning and turned toward the male voice. Recognizing her lifelong friend, she let out a sigh. "Gavin Mitchell, you scared the life right out of me."

"Did they tell you?"

Johanna studied his solemn expression. She'd never seen her friend so serious. He looked as if he'd slept as little as she had.

"No." She shook her head and sat on the bench. She patted the seat beside her. "What's wrong?"

Gavin looked out over the water. "I don't want to sit down." He gazed back at her with condemnation filling his expression. "I know you were with a man."

Johanna's heart fell inside her chest. Why would he be angry with her? Why would he talk to her as if she'd done something wrong? The dinner with Mike had been innocent and friendly. She'd learned so much about him, and he about her. She'd found a man she hoped liked her as much as she liked him. "Gavin, the dinner with Mike was perfectly innocent, and Daddy knew—"

"I don't like it."

Johanna stood and shoved her fists beside her thighs. "Gavin Mitchell, why are you acting like this? We are just friends."

"I don't want to be just friends."

As Johanna stewed on the words he'd just uttered, her heavenly Father's sunrise lifted from behind her friend. She couldn't enjoy His glory for trembling over Gavin's words.

Johanna shook her head. "That isn't true. You know it isn't true."

"I care about you, Johanna. You know I always have. I want you to marry me."

Johanna gasped and took a step away from him. Tears welled in her eyes. She hated the emotion that always flowed first from her eyes. "You don't mean that. I can tell you love my sister."

Gavin seemed taken aback by her words. His hardened shell seemed to break and he plopped onto the bench. "I've never uttered those words, Johanna."

Placing her hand over her chest, she stepped closer to

him. "But it's obvious. To everyone. Even to Amber. Even to Daddy."

Gavin closed his eyes. He looked as if the weight of every rock in Kentucky had fallen hard upon his shoulders. He wiped his face with the palm of his hand. "I'm sorry I have given that impression. It was not intentional."

"Intentional or not, we know you care about her."

She moved closer to him and reached out to touch his shoulder. He pushed her hand away and stood. Raking his fingers through his hair, he paced in front of her. "I cannot care for her."

He stopped and faced Johanna. "Look, you *are* my friend. I do have feelings for Amber, but they don't matter." He raked his fingers through his hair again. "The truth is I need to marry you."

Johanna squinted at him. "Why would you need to marry me?"

He flopped onto the bench again. "Last spring my father found out he has multiple sclerosis. He didn't want to tell anyone. His symptoms are getting worse."

He looked up at Johanna. His expression pleaded with her to understand. "We need help. The boys and I take care of the farm, but Mama needs help. She can't care for Dad and the baby and all that needs to be done."

Johanna frowned. "Gavin, you can get help. You don't have to marry."

Gavin looked away from her, his expression angry. "You know our farm doesn't make enough money to hire someone. We make it by God's grace alone."

Johanna tried to make sense of what he asked. Maybe the lack of sleep had twisted her ability to reason. Or maybe it had twisted his. "But there are so many ways to get help, and our church family can help, and— You don't love me, Gavin. You love Amber."

Gavin stood and smacked his thigh. "Is Amber going to give up going to high school? And college? Is she going to give up her dream to share God's Word through piano and song? I won't do that to her."

Johanna was stunned by the emotion in Gavin's voice. She could see that he loved Amber more than he'd even realized.

He reached for Johanna's hands, but she pulled away. "I'm sorry, Johanna. You and I *are* friends. I offer you the life you want, the life of a farmer's wife. You know I care for you. I would always be good to you."

Johanna stood still as a hunter who'd locked her gun sight onto a deer. What could she say to Gavin? How could he ask this?

Weariness fell over his face, and he shoved his hands into his front pockets. "Just think about what I've asked. I *would* always be good to you."

Johanna watched as her friend walked down the hill and toward the driveway. She'd been wrapped up in such happiness she hadn't even heard him pull up. Now, sadness draped itself upon her.

Mr. Mitchell had multiple sclerosis. She didn't know what all the disease entailed, but Gavin had said he was worsening. Poor Mrs. Mitchell. She already had her hands more than full.

Johanna knew Gavin's words were true that his mother needed help, and she knew they couldn't afford to hire help. She would help all she could, but Gavin was right, they would need more help than she could offer after work or after her own chores.

But how could she marry Gavin when she knew he had feelings for Amber and Johanna had such strong feelings for Mike? She thought of her mother telling her how she had loved another man but married her father. The idea of going through the heartbreak and then learning to love again tore at her insides.

But it was more than her heart involved. It was Gavin's, as well. And even more than that, it was Amber's. *God, I can't be the one who breaks my sister's heart.*

***

Mike's dad's voice sounded from the other side of the barn. "Well, hello there, Pastor Smith."

Stunned, Mike stopped walking and put the bag of feed he carried on the ground. *Pastor Smith? That would have to be Johanna's dad.*

"How are you?" a deeper voice responded. "I've come to see Mike if he's around."

"Didn't know you knew Mike." His dad laughed.

The other man chortled. "Well, I've been hearing a lot about him lately."

"Hope it was all good stuff."

Mike cringed. His dad loved to tease people, but the last person he wanted thinking poorly of him was Johanna's father. He sighed. *I might as well go on over to him.* He clapped his hands together, trying to get most of the dust off, and walked around the barn.

Taken aback at the size of Johanna's father, Mike raised his eyebrows. The man had to be every bit of six feet five inches and probably weighed well over two hundred pounds. He extended his hand to the huge man. "I'm Mike McCauley."

Her father smiled, and Mike noted the same dimple in his left cheek. "It's good to meet you, son. I won't keep you. I know you two have a lot of work to do, but I wanted to invite you to dinner tonight. Six o'clock."

Mike nodded. His heart sped up like a tractor going downhill out of gear. He feared it would be several days before he'd be able to see Johanna again. He'd thought about her all night. "That sounds terrific. Thank you."

Her father gave him their address and waved good-bye. His dad stared at him. "What was that about, Mike?"

"I think I've met my future wife."

His dad howled. "Your wife?"

"I'm serious, Dad." He folded the paper and put it in his front jeans pocket. "I'm going to have dinner with them tonight."

His dad squinted. "I think I'd like to meet this young lady myself."

Mike nodded. "You'll love her."

His father patted his back. "I'm sure I will."

Mike tried to focus on farmwork the rest of the day. He and his father had plenty to do, but Mike couldn't keep his mind on his work. He drove his father so crazy he finally sent him to the house to fix the loose shingles on the roof. He dropped his hammer off the roof and had to climb down and then back up—twice.

At four o'clock, his dad took mercy on him. He shooed him to his truck. "Go on home. Take a shower. Get ready to go to that gal's house. I'm afraid you're going to tear my house down if you don't get out of here."

Mike decided not to argue. He waved good-bye, hopped

in the truck, and headed for home. After a long, hot shower, he tried to shave but nicked himself three times. With pieces of tissue plastered over his bloody spots, he searched his closet for something to wear. He pulled out two different shirts and wrinkled his nose at both. *I feel like a woman. Isn't this what women do? Worry over clothes. This is what my mom does.*

Exasperated with himself, he hung up one of the shirts and stuck the other one on. He finished getting dressed, brushed his hair, then pulled the tissues off his face.

Ready to go, he started the truck and headed toward her house. Praying the entire way, he allowed the Holy Spirit to calm his heart and mind.

He'd had such a good time with Johanna the night before. He knew he had nothing to worry about. Her father seemed nice. Her mother and sisters would surely be equally as welcoming.

As he pulled into the driveway, a huge golden retriever greeted him. He hoped they didn't use him as a guard dog, because before Mike could get out of the truck the animal had already tried to lick him to death.

"Max, get down."

He looked up when he heard Johanna's voice. She looked beautiful in a light-green sundress. Her long blond hair fell in waves over her shoulders. Even from a distance, he could see the sparkle in her eyes.

He waved. "Hi, Johanna."

She waved back. "Hi, Mike."

He'd asked his mother if she would cut a small bouquet of flowers from her garden. The night before, at the café, he'd shared how much the flowers meant to his mother since his brother's death. He hoped she understood how special the gift was. He handed her the bouquet. "My mom cut this for you."

Johanna's lips formed a perfect O and she lifted them to her nose. "They're wonderful. Please tell her thank you, and that I'm honored she'd share them with me."

Mike wanted to pick the woman up and twirl her around. She did understand. She was perfect for him. He wanted to reach up and touch a strand of her hair, to feel how soft it was. He wanted to lean down and kiss her perfect lips. But those things could wait.

First, he would meet her family. He followed her up the sidewalk and into the house. Her home was warm and inviting, but it was the aroma of soup beans and corn bread coming from the kitchen that demanded his attention.

Johanna pointed to the older of her two sisters. "Mike, this is Amber." Amber smiled then Johanna pointed to the younger one. "This is Bethany."

Mike nodded and shook the older then the younger girl's hand. "It's a pleasure to meet you."

She turned toward the woman who could have easily been Johanna's twin a couple of decades before. "And this is my mother, Melissa Smith."

Mike nodded and extended his hand. She smiled and shook it, but he could tell the smile didn't quite reach her eyes. "It's a pleasure to meet you, Mrs. Smith."

"We're glad to have you, Mike." She turned toward her other children and clasped her hands. "Let's eat."

Mike followed Johanna into the dining room. The table was covered with some of the best Kentucky cooking a man could imagine. They'd fixed soup beans and homemade sauerkraut, fried potatoes, and fried green tomatoes. And the corn bread looked so fluffy that it could float off the plate. If the food tasted as good as it looked, he would ask Johanna to marry him tonight.

"It's good to see you again, Mike." Pastor Smith's voice boomed from the other side of the room.

Mike nodded. "Thank you for having me." He looked at Mrs. Smith, hoping her demeanor would soften. "The food looks delicious."

Again, she smiled, but it seemed stiff. "Thank you, Mike." She looked at her husband. "I invited another guest. I'm sure he'll be here in just a moment."

"Hello!" A man's voice sounded from the front door. "Sorry I'm late."

Mike watched as Johanna's face blanched, while Amber sat up straighter and smiled. He looked toward the door and saw a tall, dark-haired man.

"Have a seat, Gavin." Mrs. Smith pointed to the empty chair beside Amber. The woman's demeanor changed significantly in this man's presence. Mike noticed that Pastor Smith gave his wife a weary glance.

"Hello, everyone. Have I missed grace?"

"No, son. You're right on time." Pastor Smith grabbed hands with the daughter on each side of him. Mike held Johanna's hand and Bethany's. He tried not to think about how soft Johanna's hand was or how perfectly it fit in his. Her father's "amen" brought him back to reality and he released her hand, but he noticed the flush that had crept up her neck. It made him happy to know that he affected her in the same way.

They started passing the food, and Mike filled his plate

and bowl. He took a big bite of fried potatoes. They were scrumptious.

"So you must be the man Johanna had dinner with last night?"

Mike looked up at the man they'd called Gavin. "Yes. I'm Mike. It's nice to meet you."

"I think we've seen each other before."

Mike made a fist and pressed it against his mouth. "You know, I thought you looked familiar. We have a farm over in River Run. Where do you work?"

"I farm here in Hickory Hill. You're McCauley, right?"

Mike nodded. "That's right. What was your last name again?"

"Mitchell."

Mike racked his mind for where he'd heard that name before. He remembered his dad had mentioned a friend who'd gotten sick in the last year. At the time, the prognosis wasn't good. Mike's dad would have never known about it if he hadn't run into the guy when taking Mike's mother to the doctor. The man had an unusual first name. What was it? He snapped his fingers. "Is your dad's name Gorman?"

Gavin smiled. "The one and only."

Mike frowned. "How's he doing? My dad saw him last year at the doctor's office. He was worried for him."

Mike felt Johanna stiffen beside him. Gavin's face fell, and he sat back in his chair and rested his hands in his lap. "Right now, he's not doing very well."

Mrs. Smith peered at Gavin. "What's wrong with your dad?"

Pastor Smith also looked concerned. "Son, is something the matter with Gorman?"

Gavin stood and pushed his chair under the table. "I'm

sorry. I'd best be going. I know I'm needed at home."

Gavin stared at Johanna, and Mike glanced at her to see if she understood the meaning behind Gavin's look. She averted her gaze to her plate, but the pain in her expression was apparent.

Gavin headed toward the door, and Pastor Smith followed him. After a few moments, Johanna's father returned and told them Gavin shared that his father had multiple sclerosis.

Mike felt horrible. No one had known. He hadn't meant to tell a family secret. He hadn't meant to upset Gavin and Johanna's family. They ate in silence, but everyone seemed finished long before their plates were empty.

Pastor Smith was the first to speak. "Amber and Bethany, you do the dishes." He nodded to Johanna. "Why don't you and Mike go for a walk? It's a beautiful evening."

Mike followed Johanna out the back door. "I'm sorry about that."

Johanna shook her head. "Don't be upset. You didn't know."

Mike studied her. "But you did?"

She nodded. "Gavin just told me today." She surprised him when she grabbed his hand. "May I show you something?"

Mike intertwined his fingers through hers. He didn't want her to let go. Her soft hand belonged in his. "Absolutely."

She guided him up a small hill. At the top sat a bench that overlooked a huge pond. "Johanna, this is beautiful."

She released his hand and sat on the bench. He watched how the fading sunlight shone through each strand of her hair. She was more beautiful than he knew how to describe.

Crossing her legs, she peered up at him. "This is where I spend time with God."

He sat down beside her and took her hand in his. She didn't pull away. "It's a perfect place."

She sneaked a peek at him. "I prayed about you in this spot this morning."

"I prayed about you a few times today, as well."

She laughed and brushed a strand of hair behind her ear with her free hand. "I like you, Mike McCauley."

"I like you, too, Johanna Smith. Very much."

She stared out at the water, and he studied her profile for just a few moments longer. Lifting his eyes to the sky, he smiled into the heavens. *God, thank You for bringing her into my life. I'm going to make her my wife.*

eleven

Johanna shelved another book in its proper spot. She hadn't seen Gavin for three weeks. Their family hadn't even attended church. She knew her father had visited the Mitchells' house several times. Her mother and Amber had also gone to help. Johanna had offered to clean or do laundry with Mrs. Mitchell, but her father always had something else for her to do. And he'd invited Mike for dinner at least three evenings a week.

Not that she minded.

When Johanna thought of Mike McCauley, her heart beat faster and her knees grew weak. As she picked up another book to shelve, she took in the man and woman on the cover. They looked at each other longingly. Obviously a romance. All the emotions she'd always believed to be ridiculous fancies in those kinds of books and movies now filled her with joy and wonder. She knew, whether ridiculous or not, the feelings were true and powerful.

A young boy poked her arm. She recognized him as the student who hadn't wanted to visit her station at the "Spring into a Good Book" event just a few months ago. She smiled down at the dark-haired child. He'd grown even taller since she'd last seen him. "Hi. How is your summer going?"

"Fine." He pushed his jaw forward and pointed at an empty place between two teeth. "Lost my first tooth yesterday."

Johanna clapped. "Congratulations. You're growing up."

"Got a dollar from the tooth fairy." He pointed to a woman holding a toddler and perusing the newly released novels. "That's my mom over there."

Johanna nodded.

"I'm going to first grade this year."

"Are you excited?"

He shrugged. "I don't know. School is school." He looked at the children's section. "You wanna read me another book? Another one about farming maybe?"

Pride welled within her. He'd been quite a handful during the event the past spring, and she wondered if he struggled with literacy when she'd read the book, and he'd had a hard time responding when it called for the students to help her finish some of the sentences. But he had still enjoyed himself, and she wanted to encourage him to read. She reached out her hand and he grabbed hold of it. "Let's go pick one out."

"Mom," he yelled and pointed to Johanna. His mother looked up. "She's the library lady. She's going to read a book to me."

Her cheeks warmed when everyone in the library peered at them. His mother simply nodded and gazed back at the books.

Johanna whispered, "Remember to use a quiet voice in the library."

"Okay," he boomed in a voice almost as quiet as a lion threatened by an enemy.

Shaking her head, she guided him to the children's section. She couldn't remember the child's name, so she pointed to her chest. "Do you remember my name is Johanna?"

He nodded. "Yeah, and I'm Hunter in case you forgot."

"I had forgotten, Hunter. Thank you for reminding me."

They picked out a farming book and then settled onto the plush, shag rug. She read several sentences then encouraged him to read the easy words like "sat" and "cat" and "dog."

Just as she suspected, he struggled to sound out the words. Only going into first grade, she knew he wouldn't be a proficient reader, but he should have been able to identify letters and their sounds.

When they finished the book, Hunter grabbed another book off the shelf. This one, about cars. She read that book then he grabbed another. After almost half an hour and several more books, Johanna looked around the library to spy his mother. The woman sat in an overstuffed chair in the fiction section reading a book. The toddler draped over her shoulder, obviously asleep.

Hunter had grown weary of reading books, but Johanna figured his mother most likely wanted her little one to rest a bit longer. She looked at her watch, but she needed to get back to work. An idea popped into her head. She pointed to a stack of books on the front desk. "Hunter, would you like to help me put those away?"

He wrinkled his nose and shrugged. "I guess."

Noting the less than enthusiastic tone in his voice, she added, "It'll take someone pretty strong to help me out. You'll have to hold several books at a time."

Jutting out his chin, he lifted his arm and bent his elbow, making a muscle. "I'm super strong. Feel it."

Johanna wrapped her hand around the small bump and nodded. "You're right. I think you can handle it."

Hunter jumped up to a standing position. He spotted his mother and yelled, "Hey, Mom. Johanna needs someone strong. So I'm gonna help her."

His mother nodded as she laid the book in her lap and with her free hand placed her pointer finger over her lips to remind him to be quiet. She gazed at Johanna and mouthed, "Thank you."

Johanna walked Hunter to the front desk. She loaded six big books in his arms and motioned for him to follow her to the nonfiction section. It seemed to take much longer to put back all the books with Hunter's help, but he had such a good time she couldn't bear to finish without him.

His sister finally awakened, and his mother found them and told Hunter they needed to leave. Johanna knelt down in front of the child and shook his hand. "Thank you for all your hard work. You were a big help." She snapped her fingers. "I think I've got a sucker in the back. Would you like one?"

Hunter nodded, and Johanna realized she hadn't consulted with his mother. She looked at her. "I'm sorry, I should have asked you first."

Her mother swatted the air. "No, that's fine. This is the best library trip we've had in a long time."

Johanna nodded and raced to the break area. Pulling out two suckers from the leftover candy for the last children's event, she walked back out. Her heartbeat sped up when she saw Mike standing at the front desk. Hunter and his mother and sister stood next to him. She handed a sucker to Hunter and then asked his mother if the toddler could have one as well.

She nodded, and the little girl squealed with delight when Johanna handed the child-safe sucker to her. Hunter whined, "That's not fair. She didn't do any work."

Johanna gazed at Hunter. "But she took a good long nap so that you could help out."

Hunter pinched his lips. Johanna could almost see the little wheels churning in his head as he contemplated if he would accept that as a viable reason to give her a sucker. Finally, he nodded. "Okay."

His mother grabbed his hand, and Johanna watched as they walked out the door. She couldn't hold back a smile when she looked into Mike's eyes.

"You're really good with kids."

"I love kids."

"It's obvious."

Before she could respond, Mrs. Love raced up beside her and said, "I can't believe the library is still intact." She pulled a tissue from her front pocket and patted her nose. "Every week this summer, usually on Tuesdays when you aren't here, that woman brings that boy into the library. He runs around like a maniac, and she just sits in a corner reading a book."

A need to defend Hunter welled up inside her. Obviously loud and sometimes difficult to deal with, mainly he was just inquisitive and bored easily and needed someone to give him one-on-one attention. He also loved to help. "He helped out a lot today."

Mrs. Love placed a hand on her chest. "I know it. I don't know how you did it, Johanna. The boy frazzles my nerves. Hopefully, she'll start coming on days when you're here."

"I hope so."

Mrs. Love walked away, and Johanna turned back toward Mike. It bothered her that her boss grew so perturbed with children who didn't sit silently with their hands folded in their laps. "He's really not so bad. He just likes attention and likes to keep moving."

Adoration gleamed from Mike's eyes, and heat swelled in Johanna's cheeks. "You are amazing, Johanna Smith."

She averted her gaze. "Not really."

"I would disagree, but I came to ask you if you'll have dinner with my family tonight. My parents are anxious to meet you."

Nervousness twisted her stomach. "Well, sure. I'll need to call Mama—"

"I've already talked with your dad. He said it's fine."

Johanna nodded. Her chest tightened and her stomach muscles twisted some more. "Okay."

Mike placed his hand on hers. "Don't be nervous. My parents will love you. You may even be the breath of fresh air my mother needs." He winked. "You've been good for me."

Johanna ducked her chin at his praise. Her feelings for Mike had deepened over the last weeks. Her father especially liked Mike and encouraged their relationship to blossom. *But Daddy doesn't know what Gavin asked me. He doesn't know they need permanent help.* She pushed the thought away.

Gavin hadn't returned any of her calls. Her heart yearned for Mike, not Gavin. And her mind couldn't quite wrap around the notion of marrying Gavin because he needed help. Even though her sister was too young and wanted to finish high school and college, and it would be possibly years before Amber was ready to settle down—there were simply no circumstances under which Johanna could accept the idea of marrying a man who loved Amber and whom Amber adored.

&

With dinner finished and after he and his father had cleaned up the kitchen, Mike lowered into one of the wicker chairs on the front porch. His dad swung in the wooden swing beside him. He watched as Johanna knelt with his mother beside one of her favorite flower gardens. His mother took great pride in the various patches of flowers she'd planted around the front and back yards. Together, they inspected her most recent creation.

Johanna laughed at something his mother said, and his mom smiled the first genuine smile he'd seen in a long time. Johanna pointed at something, and his mother's face grew animated as she responded.

"She's a really nice girl, Mike."

"Yes. I think so."

"So, how serious are you?"

Mike took a long drink of his sweetened iced tea. He stole his gaze away from Johanna and peered at his father. "I want to marry her. Just like I said before."

His father's eyes twinkled. "I thought you might still feel that way."

"You disapprove?"

"Absolutely not. I've known her father for years. He's an honest Christian man. From everything I've seen from her, she shares all of her father's good qualities." He glanced at Mike. "Have you spoken with her dad?"

Mike leaned forward and rested his elbows on his knees. "Not yet. I've only been seeing her a little over a month."

His father pushed the swing back then turned and spit off the side of the porch. "Let me tell you a little bit about her dad. Roger Smith is extremely conservative in his beliefs. Some would even call him old-fashioned. He would appreciate knowing your intentions, and he wouldn't tell Johanna."

Mike pondered his father's advice until he noticed Johanna motioning for them to join her and his mother. He got up and stepped off the porch. "I'll think about that, Dad."

His mother started motioning for them to join them.

"What is it?" his father called.

"Johanna is begging me to take a walk." His mother acted exasperated, but her face shone brighter than it had in almost a year. "I told her I'd go only if you two went with us."

Johanna stuck out her bottom lip and batted her eyes at him and his father.

Mike laughed. "If you're going to make us."

Johanna clapped her hands like a schoolgirl. His dad reached his mother, took her hand in his, and led her onto the gravel road. Mike wanted to hold Johanna's hand. They had for a brief moment the first time she'd showed him her favorite worship spot by the pond. He still wasn't convinced she realized she'd held his hand then, or if she'd just been wrapped up in the moment. A war raged within him as he battled if he should try to hold her hand.

McCauley, the worst thing she can do is pull her hand away. He inwardly chastised himself. Grabbing her hand, he intertwined his fingers with hers. She didn't pull away. He sneaked a peek at her and noticed her neck and cheeks bloomed red. He held their joined hands up. "Is this okay?"

She peered up at him and nodded then averted her gaze.

"You know you're awfully cute when your face turns red."

Johanna gasped and punched his arm with her free hand. "Mike McCauley."

"What?" He feigned hurt and innocence. "You're cute when you aren't embarrassed, too."

She stomped her foot. "Mike."

He laughed out loud. His parents turned around to look at them then turned back around and continued their conversation.

He pointed ahead. "Look, you worried my parents."

"Mike McCauley," she hissed. "Stop teasing me or I'm pulling my hand away."

He sobered. "Don't do that. Your hand is so soft and fits perfectly with mine."

She ducked her head. "Okay."

They walked together in silence. Mike peered at his and his father's farm. If Johanna would have him as a husband, it would be her farm as well. They would work alongside each other. Their children and grandchildren would play in these fields. He'd always been a simple man, longing for a simple life. Not an easy one. He'd spend the rest of his days doing hard work. But he wanted someone to share his life with. Someone with long blond hair and a sparkle to her green-with-flecks-of-brown eyes. And that dimple in her left cheek. He wanted Johanna.

twelve

Johanna tossed the cell phone in the passenger's seat beside her. She'd had it with Gavin Mitchell. It had been over a month since he'd interrupted her quiet time and announced she had to marry him because he needed help. Though head over heels in love with Mike, she seemed to dwell in some weird love triangle that Mike didn't even know existed because of what Gavin had asked.

Furious, she turned onto the blacktop road that led to Gavin's house. Normally, she enjoyed the beauty of the drive to the Mitchell home. Overwhelmed with frustration at this moment, she needed closure. Today.

She wanted to tell Gavin to forget it, that he'd stepped way out of line asking for her hand in marriage the way he had. They didn't live in the eighteenth or even the nineteenth century. There were ways for his family to get the assistance they needed. His pride alone made him feel he *had* to marry. If his mother knew what he'd asked of her, knowing he cared for her sister, she'd find his old time-out chair and sit him in a corner.

And what kind of life would his wife of duty or convenience— or whatever he chose to call it—have? Versions of the old play and movie, *Seven Brides for Seven Brothers*, danced through her mind. Adam had essentially tricked poor Millie into marrying him. He'd only wanted a wife to care for him and his brood of brothers. *Hmm. Actually, it sounds very similar.*

She'd had plenty of time to stew on Gavin's request. Everything in her wanted to punch him in the nose. How dare he think that he could ask for her hand after admitting he loved her sister? "Ugh!" She smacked the top of the steering wheel.

Her frustration with Gavin had grown the last few days, as Johanna realized how deep her feelings for Mike were becoming. Amber, who was ready to start her senior year of high school in only a few weeks, still spoke privately with Johanna about her feelings for Gavin.

She turned the last right that led to his driveway. As she drove up, she spied two of the middle boys pushing each other in a tire swing hung from the old maple tree in the front yard. One of the younger ones played in a sandbox. The baby slept in a playpen under a shade tree. Mrs. Mitchell hung clothes on the line a few yards away.

When they heard her car wheels crunching on the gravel, the boys hopped off the swing and out of the sandbox and raced toward her. Mrs. Mitchell waved.

The love Johanna felt for this, her second family, filled her heart. She hugged the boys and then walked over to Gavin's mother. The older woman wrapped her arms around Johanna, and Johanna knew she would be the kindest mother-in-law ever. "What a pleasure to see you, honey. What brings you out here?"

"I'm actually here to find Gavin."

His mother pointed to the barn. "He should be about done working for the day."

Johanna nodded to the clothes. "After I talk with him, I'd love to help you with these."

Mrs. Mitchell swatted at her. "Nonsense. I'm almost

finished. You go find Gavin."

Johanna peered into the eyes of the woman who'd always been like a second mother to her. "How's Mr. Mitchell?"

She smiled and her eyes lit up. "He's on some medicine that is really helping him. He's actually in the barn with the boys."

Johanna hugged the woman again. "I'm so happy to hear that."

The older woman wiped a tear from beneath her eye and sniffed. "Me too, sweetie." She nudged Johanna's arm. "Go find Gavin."

Thanksgiving swelled in Johanna's heart that Gavin's father was doing well. She lifted up a prayer of gratitude as she made her way to the barn and heard several of the Mitchell men talking. It did sound as if they were about to finish up for the day. "Hello!" Johanna called before she reached the front of the barn.

Eighteen-year-old Gabe stuck his head out from inside the barn. "Hey, Johanna. What brings you out here?"

"Looking for Gavin."

"Oh," Gabe grunted then scrunched up his face. "Don't know"—he lifted his leg and rubbed the back of it as if someone had just kicked him—"where he is."

Johanna crossed her arms in front of her chest. "I heard you talking, Gavin. Get out here."

His father's "Hee-haw" sounded from inside the barn. "I told you she wouldn't fall for no fibs."

Johanna couldn't hold back a grin. Mr. Mitchell remained as mischievous as the day was long. He shouldn't have allowed his son to try to fib to her, but the older man knew how to bring a lot of laughter to his home.

Gavin walked out of the barn, his head hung low. He peeked

up at her like a pup that begged for mercy for messing on the floor.

She motioned for him to follow her. "We need to talk."

They walked several yards to the gazebo his father had built for his mother. He'd even dug her a decorative pond and put koi fish inside. Mrs. Mitchell told them it was her place to escape the chaos of all her men.

Johanna sat on the bench inside and looked up at her friend. His dark hair fell in his eyes. In desperate need of a haircut, he appeared to have missed a shave or two in the last few days as well. "Why haven't you returned my calls?"

Gavin stepped inside the gazebo and leaned against the rail. He folded his arms in front of his chest. There was no denying Gavin was a handsome man. A man whose broad shoulders and tall stature exhibited strength. Much like her father, he was big as a bear. "I guess you thought about what I asked you."

Johanna spread out her arms. "Of course I've thought about what you asked me. I haven't been able to get it out of my mind." She stood and poked him in the chest. "But you wouldn't return my calls."

He stood up straight and puffed out his chest. "What's your answer?"

Her mouth fell open. How could he possibly still want to marry her? She rubbed her eyes with her hands. She knew her mother had fallen in love with her father after they were married. She knew Gavin was a faithful and true friend, who loved the Lord. But she also knew her sister cared deeply for this man, and that Johanna loved Mike. She couldn't do it. Smacking her hands against her thighs, she released a growl. She simply couldn't do it. "The answer is no."

She pointed her finger at him. "I can't believe you would

ask—" Gavin released a long sigh and wrapped his arms around her. She pushed him away. "What are you doing? I said no."

"I know." He laughed and sat on the bench. "I've avoided you because I felt miserable for what I asked. It was wrong of me."

Frustration of a new kind swelled within her. "So, you just avoided me? Let me stew about what you asked? And not even tell me you were wrong?"

Gavin shrugged. "Really, I'm surprised you're here. I knew you were spending a lot of time with Mike. I knew your dad approved of him. I figured you hadn't given any more thought to what I said that morning. At least, I hoped you hadn't. I decided if I stayed away you'd know I should have never asked in the first place."

Johanna bit the inside of her lip as she contemplated whether or not she should pummel the man. "Gavin, we've been friends since birth. You shouldn't have avoided me."

"You're right. I'm sorry."

Johanna huffed and stomped her foot. "You're sorry, and that's supposed to make everything all right?"

He looked at her and stuck out his bottom lip. "Pwease."

She snarled at him. "Are you kidding me? You're a grown man." She punched his shoulder. "Don't act like that."

He winced and grabbed his shoulder, even though she knew he'd probably only barely felt her punch. "Does that mean you forgive me?"

Johanna blew out a breath. "Of course I forgive you."

He hopped off the seat and gave her a hug. "I knew you'd forgive me." He stepped off the gazebo and started heading toward her car. "You're right about me liking your sister."

"She definitely likes you, too."

"So maybe we'll be related one day anyway."

Johanna snorted. "I really ought to kick your behind for making me worry about this all month."

Gavin placed his hand against his chest. "I'd have never dreamed you were so uptight about things."

She swatted his arm again. "You know I'm uptight about things."

He opened the car door for her. "Well, I am sorry. Truly."

Realizing they'd walked through the yard and hadn't seen a single member of his family, she looked toward the house. "Where is everyone?"

He peered at his watch. "It's five o'clock. *Happy Days* reruns are on. Would you believe every Mitchell in the family loves to watch *Happy Days*?"

Johanna rolled her eyes and slipped into the car. "You all are crazy."

He shut the door and tapped the hood. "Yep. I better go, 'cause I'm missing it."

He waited while she started the car and drove off. In the rearview mirror, she saw him skip into the house. He was crazy, and she should be livid with him. But all she could think about was she was free to love Mike.

☙

Mike pushed OFF on his cell phone. He'd waited until mid-August to ask Johanna's father to his house. After talking with his own father the first night Johanna had eaten dinner with them, Mike decided he wanted to fix up his house before asking her father for her hand in marriage. He had more insulation put in and new windows installed. Both of which made a huge mess, so Addy helped him with coloring up the place. With her being six months pregnant, Nick wouldn't let her do any of the work. But she picked out all the colors, and he and his friends did all the painting.

Once he finally got the house all ready it was the beginning of August, and Amber started school. Their whole family had been as anxious as a heifer whose calf was turning a week or two before birthing time. He'd decided to wait another week. Addy's aunt Becky came out and cleaned the house up real good for him.

His mother had even come over and worked a bit on his landscape. Though she'd only attended one time, his mom had even visited a Sunday evening service with him and his dad at Johanna's church.

He paced the living room floor, trying to remember all he wanted to say. Everything in and around the house smelled good and looked good. Now, he just had to wait for Pastor Smith to show up.

Crunching gravel sounded from outside the house. Mike peered out the window and saw that Pastor Smith had arrived. He exhaled a nervous breath. *God, give me the right words to say. I believe Pastor Smith respects me, but I want him to know that with me his daughter will be loved, protected, and cared for.*

Mike opened the front door before Johanna's father made it up the porch. He nodded and extended his hand. "Evening. Thanks for taking the time to come out and see me."

Pastor Smith shook his hand. "Anytime, son."

Mike stepped outside and shut the screen door. "If you don't mind, I'd like to show you around my property first."

A smile tugged at Pastor Smith's mouth, but he nodded. "Go right ahead, son."

He tried to keep his hands clasped, as they simply would not stop shaking. It was too far to walk to the barn near his parents' house, but he pointed out the farm's boundary lines and explained where the cattle grazed.

Taking Pastor Smith inside the house, he showed him the improvements he'd made—the new windows and insulation, the plumbing and floors. Mike pointed to the kitchen cabinets. "I know these are a bit old, but I wanted to wait until. . ." His face warmed. He almost said he wanted to let Johanna pick out cabinets she'd like.

Pastor Smith cupped his chin. "Until what, son?"

Mike blew out a deep breath. "Could I get you a soft drink?"

Pastor Smith nodded. "Sure." He pointed to the kitchen table. "Would you like me to have a seat?"

Mike pulled two drinks out of the refrigerator and handed one to Johanna's father. "That would be great."

Mike sat opposite Pastor Smith. He wrapped his fingers around the can, allowing the coldness to calm his nerves. Mike studied the older man across from him. It was obvious Pastor Smith knew Mike's intentions. Still, Mike wanted to assure him that he would care for Johanna.

Mike opened the soft drink and took a quick swig. "I know you know why I've asked you here."

Pastor Smith rested his hand on top of the table. "Why have you asked me here?"

"I'd like to request your daughter's hand in marriage."

"Which one?"

Mike furrowed his brows and gawked at the older gentleman. Had he lost his mind? Which one?

Pastor Smith let out a loud belly laugh. He smacked the tabletop. "I'm assuming you mean Johanna."

Mike laughed as well. "Yes, I mean Johanna."

"It's about time you finally asked me."

"I had planned to ask earlier but I wanted to get some things fixed around the house, and then Amber started school. I had to wait for the right time."

Pastor Smith extended his hand, and Mike accepted the handshake. "I will be proud to have you as a son-in-law. So when will you be asking Johanna?"

"I plan to take her on a picnic at your house this weekend."

A confused expression wrapped Pastor Smith's features.

Mike continued, "I'd like to propose at your pond."

The older man opened his mouth and nodded. "Oh, good idea." He snapped then pointed his finger at Mike. "Smart man. She'll love that."

"I hope so." Mike didn't tell him about the other half of his surprise. He wanted it to be solely between Johanna and him.

Pastor Smith stood up and pulled his truck keys from his front pocket. "Your house and farm are very nice, Mike. I know you'll take good care of my daughter." He shook the keys. "But I best be going before they start wondering why their old man is so late for dinner."

Mike followed his guest to the door then walked back to his bedroom and opened the top dresser drawer. He pulled out the small box and popped it open. The ring he'd bought a few weeks ago was perfect. When he saw it, he immediately thought of Johanna. A gold band and a small circular diamond. Just like her, it was simple, but beautiful. Shutting the lid, he tucked it inside the drawer again. The weekend couldn't arrive fast enough.

thirteen

Johanna slipped into her sweatpants and old shoes. She looked at her sister and her mother, who'd also donned their old clothes. "Mama, you get the flashlights?"

Her mom lifted them up. "Got them right here."

Johanna took one from her mother, as did Amber. Since the first time she went frog gigging, Amber never allowed Johanna and her mother to go without her.

Amber pointed outside. "I laid the gigs against the house."

With gear in hand, the three made the quick trek to the pond. Amber had yet to spear a bullfrog, though there were definitely more to be had the closer it got to fall; but she excelled at hearing their sometimes muffled *varuump* and then flashing the light in their eyes to stun them.

"Amber, how was school today?" Her mother's voice sounded from a few feet behind Johanna.

Amber huffed. "Mom, are we going to get some bullfrogs or are we gonna talk?"

"I'd like to do both."

Johanna backed up her sister. "Let's finish gigging then we'll talk."

Her mother nodded, and the three turned their attention to the sounds of the night, most specifically their prey. Time passed quickly, and soon they were sitting side by side on Johanna's favorite bench with an onion sack filled with fifteen bullfrogs on the ground beside them.

Johanna stared at the full moon that draped its beauty on the still pond waters. Trees of various sizes and shapes stood majestically in the distance. The occasional call of a bullfrog and the constant chirps of crickets calmed her spirit.

She looked at their mud-caked shoes and legs. Their arms and hands were filthy, but happiness filled her that she could share this moment with her mother and sister.

Her mom, who sat in the middle of them, nudged Amber's shoulder. "So how was school today?"

"It was good. Mrs. Watkins is really helping me with my math. I'm still behind, but I've met a friend. Her name is Hannah, and she's helping me, too."

"That's wonderful, Amber." The relief in her mother's tone was evident, and Johanna knew her parents still prayed that they'd made the right choice for her sister.

Johanna cleared her throat. "Mike is coming over tomorrow."

"I know it," her mother said.

Johanna frowned. "How do you know it? He only just asked me today."

"I think your daddy told me."

"But I haven't told Daddy."

Her mother shrugged. "Then I have no idea."

Amber interrupted their conversation. "Gavin's coming, too."

"I knew that as well." She turned toward Johanna.

"See, your father must have asked the boys to come first."

Johanna bit the inside of her lips. Maybe that was possible. She'd thought he'd asked her in such a way that he wanted her to be sure it was okay with her family, but maybe she was imagining things.

Her mother and Amber started talking about Gavin, and Johanna found her mind wandering. She was thankful her mother had figured out on her own about Amber's and Gavin's feelings for each other. There would be no more trying to talk Johanna into having romantic fancies for her childhood friend.

But she hadn't seen Gavin since the day she stopped at his house. She'd forgiven him, but a niggling of frustration with him still bit at her gut. To her knowledge, Mike hadn't seen Gavin since that day they'd had dinner together—the day Mike accidentally told the family about his father's illness. She wondered how Mike would feel about spending time with Gavin.

"I can't help but wonder when Mike will finally propose to Johanna." Amber's voice broke her concentration.

She gaped at her sister. "What?"

Her sister lifted her hands. "What's it been? Two and a half or three months?"

"Amber." Johanna stood and placed her hands on her hips. "I can't believe you would say that."

Her mother giggled, and Johanna gaped at her as well. "Mama."

Her mother shrugged. "Johanna, it's pretty obvious to the rest of us that you are head over heels for Mike." She leaned forward. "And I believe he feels the same about you."

Johanna placed her hands over her chest. She didn't want to talk about this with them. Her heart yearned for him to ask her to be his wife. She knew they'd known each other only a short time, but their faith, their desires, their personalities fit so perfectly. Still, she did not want to share that with her mother and her sister. At least not at the same time. Maybe in the confines of the house, where a perfect stranger couldn't meander up to them and hear their conversation. Or a dear friend, the way Gavin had surprised her one day.

Her mother stood up and stretched her back. With one last giggle, she motioned toward the house. "Amber, let's stop teasing Johanna and head back to the house. We still have to clean our frogs."

Amber groaned. "This is the part I hate."

Johanna followed a small distance behind her mother and sister. Now she wouldn't be able to sleep the whole night because she'd be dreaming of Mike asking her to marry him.

❧

Mike patted his front jeans pocket for what must have been the hundredth time. Nervousness and anticipation warred within him. He'd planned to take her for a picnic lunch at her pond, but she, her sisters, and her mother changed the plans since they'd gone frog gigging, yet again, the night before.

He chuckled inwardly. Those women frog gigged more than any man he knew. The delicious aroma of frying frog legs wafted through the living room where he sat, only somewhat watching the Reds game, with Pastor Smith. Normally, he'd jump at the opportunity to eat the Smith women's frog legs and fixings. Today, he just wanted the four of them to hurry up.

The older man leaned forward in his chair. He rested his hand on the side of his mouth and whispered. "I didn't know they were going to switch plans."

"It's okay. I can wait until we eat." He rolled up the magazine he'd brought with him and tapped it against his leg.

Pastor Smith furrowed his brows. "Whatcha got there?"

Praying Johanna's father wouldn't ask any more questions, he unrolled it and showed him the cover. "Just a fishing magazine."

"I believe that one is Johanna's favorite."

Mike nodded. "I think you're right."

"I'm here."

A man's voice sounded from the other room. Pastor Smith pushed himself up to his feet. "There's Gavin. He's come for lunch as well."

Mike stood and followed the older man into the kitchen. Unsure what to say after the last time he'd seen Gavin, Mike cleared his throat and extended his hand.

Gavin smiled and grabbed it in a firm handshake. "It's nice to see you again, Mike. My dad's on some medicine, and he's doing much better."

Relief washed through Mike. Already nervous enough, he didn't need the added concern of eating with a guy who was frustrated with him.

They sat down at the table, and Pastor Smith said grace over their food. Mike wanted to dig into the fried frog legs, mashed potatoes, green beans, coleslaw, and corn bread. It all looked so good, and he put a spoonful of everything on his plate, but he only ate a few bites.

Mrs. Smith rested the fork on the side of her plate. "Mike, are you ill? You've hardly touched your food." She pointed to her husband. "Usually you eat more frog legs than Roger."

Mike took a small drink of his soft drink. "Actually, I do feel a bit queasy." There was no lie in what he said. The ring in his front pocket seemed to burn a hole in his leg, and he feared at any minute he would be sick from anxiety. He pulled at his shirt collar. And, it was really hot in the dining room for some reason.

Johanna looked at him. "Mike, you do look pale."

Pastor Smith motioned out the window. "Maybe you need some fresh air, son."

Mike nodded. "Good idea." He placed his napkin beside his plate and excused himself.

He walked into the kitchen and heard Pastor Smith say, "Johanna, why don't you go and make sure he's okay?"

Mike grinned. His soon-to-be father-in-law was a smart man. Johanna walked up beside him and touched his cheek with the back of her hand. His cheek blazed at her touch and he grabbed her hand in his. "Let's take a walk."

He walked back to the living room, grabbed the magazine, then guided her out the back door. They didn't talk as they headed up the hill to Johanna's favorite worship place. Once he reached the bench, he sat and patted the seat beside him for her to follow.

Johanna studied him. "You don't look so sick anymore."

"The fresh air cured me."

He opened the magazine to the last article he'd written. "Have you read John James's article this month yet?"

Johanna nodded. "I read it at the library on Wednesday." She pointed to the author's name. "Mike, I am telling you that man lives near us."

Mike bit back a laugh. "I haven't had a chance to read this month's issue." Which was technically true since he hadn't read the other articles yet. "What's it about?"

Johanna took the magazine out of his hand. "He talks about his favorite pond."

"Tell me about it."

"Okay. First, he talked about how when he sits on his favorite bench, the pond kind of looks like a jagged half moon." She lifted her hand and swiped it slowly in front of her. "Then he talks about how the thick green grass grows just beyond it with a large hill lifting up on his left and a small hill on his right."

She paused and looked down at the magazine. "Then he talks about. . ." She frowned and skimmed the page. "He talks about three pine trees that sit kind of off by themselves on the left." She glanced up then her jaw dropped and she turned toward Mike. She pointed at the article. "John James is describing my pond. But that doesn't make—"

Mike wrinkled his nose. "Well, I would have bought some bushy gray eyebrows and a beard for you, but I just thought they'd be uncomfortable."

Johanna stared at him for a few moments then she stood and swatted his leg then his arm with the rolled-up magazine. "Mike McCauley, you are John James?"

He lifted his hands in surrender. "I confess. I confess."

She smiled and her eyes shone. "I can't believe you didn't tell me."

He patted the bench, and she sat down beside him again. "I haven't told anyone. You're the first to know." He shrugged. "Except my parents."

She peered down at the article then back at him. "You're my favorite writer."

His heart swelled. "I know, and you have no idea how happy that makes me."

She shook her hands and a disgusted look distorted her face. "To think I've held hands with a grandpa."

Mike laughed and grabbed her hand in his. He kissed her knuckles. "And you're going to hold hands with me for a long time to come."

He started to reach for the ring box when his cell phone rang. To shut it off, he pulled it out of his back pocket and accidentally hit the TALK button. He barely recognized Drew's frantic voice. He lifted the phone to his ear. Drew screamed into the phone. "Mike! Mike!"

"I'm here, man. What's wrong?"

"It's Addy. She's gone into labor. They can't stop it. The baby's too early. It's bad." Drew's voice cracked. "She's my sister, man."

"I'm coming." Mike grabbed Johanna's hand, and she stood. "Where is she?"

"On her way to the hospital. Hurry, Mike."

The phone went dead, and Mike held Johanna's hand while he raced down the hill. "Addy's in labor."

"It's too early, isn't it?"

Mike nodded. "I've got to get to the hospital."

"I'll go with you."

He looked at Johanna then wrapped his arms around her.

If she were the one in trouble. . . If it were their baby. . . He couldn't even think it. He whispered into her ear. "Thank you, Johanna."

They raced inside the house. Pastor Smith wore a smile that nearly split his face. Mike shook his head. "My friend's wife has gone into labor. It's too early."

"I'm going with him," Johanna said. "Pray for Addy and the baby."

They hopped in the truck and headed down the road. *God, this isn't how I planned this day. Have mercy on Addy and the baby.*

⋅⋅⋅

"How far along is she?" Johanna asked Gracie, the woman she'd just met.

Even though obviously fatigued, the woman had adorable short blond hair and deep-blue eyes. Gracie cuddled her own fairly new baby against her chest. "Thirty weeks."

"Her water broke," added Melody, the woman who Johanna

discovered had just married Drew. She pushed a long strand of dark-brown hair behind her ear. "They can't stop it."

Gracie shook her head then brushed a tear away from her eye. "I've got to call Mom and check on Wyatt Jr."

Swaying to keep the baby content, Gracie walked to the far wall of the hospital waiting room and pulled a cell phone out of her pocket.

"She has an eighteen-month-old at her mom's house."

Johanna turned toward Melody when she spoke. The tiny woman covered her face with her hand. "Drew is beside himself." She started to cry. "I've never seen him so scared. And Addy. . . And the baby. . . Nick."

Johanna pulled the woman into a hug.

Melody heaved as she said, "And both of their parents are gone on vacation. Together." She sniffed. "No one expected this to happen."

Johanna raked her fingers through Melody's hair. "We're going to pray for them. Lots of babies live when they're born at thirty weeks."

Melody shook her head. "Addy's baby was already small. They were monitoring him because he wasn't growing right. Or her. I don't even know if I have a niece or a nephew."

Gracie returned and wrapped her arms around Johanna and Melody. Johanna spied Mike and Wyatt to her right and motioned for them to come over. Wyatt wrapped his arms around Gracie and his baby. Johanna glanced at Mike. "Why don't we pray together?"

Melody sniffed and wiped the tears from her eyes with the back of her hand. "Johanna's right. We need to pray."

Johanna grabbed Melody's hand then took hold of Mike's. They all joined hands and bowed their heads.

"They kicked me out!"

Johanna looked up to see the man who had to be Addy's brother, Drew. Melody pulled away from Johanna's hand and wrapped her arms around her husband. He pulled her close to him. "My baby sister is in trouble, and they kicked me out."

Melody grabbed his hand and led him to the group. "Drew, we're going to pray together. It's the most powerful thing we can do."

"I can't pray right now." Drew's voice sounded panicked, and Johanna felt sure he wanted to run to the back and storm the delivery room.

"I'm going to pray," Mike commanded in a calm voice. "We all know God is bigger than this."

Peace swelled within her heart at Mike's words. She felt the collective calm that touched each of them. With every word of praise that Mike uttered, with every promise of God that Mike repeated, Johanna found herself basking in God's sovereignty and mercy.

"We ask you to save the little one Addy is delivering. The child is precious to us already. We know You are sovereign. We know Your will is best, but Jesus, we ask, we petition Your throne for mercy for this baby and for Addy."

Tears slipped down Johanna's cheeks at the urgency and honesty and pleading in Mike's voice. His words and tone were genuine, and a joy she couldn't explain even in her mind filled her to be petitioning her Father alongside this man.

He didn't stop praying. He quoted scriptures of peace and mercy. He reminded God, though He would never need reminding, that His Word promised where two or three were gathered, He would be there. And He was.

When Mike finally uttered an amen, the group sat down

together in the waiting room. Mike sat beside her and held her hand. He squeezed it gently and whispered, "This is not how I planned to spend today." He kissed her knuckles, sending butterflies through her stomach and down her legs. "I'm glad you're here with me."

Johanna wouldn't have been anywhere else.

Time dragged by as they waited for an update. Hour toppled upon hour. Every once in a while, Drew grew anxious and asked the receptionist if she'd had any updates. The woman would assure him she hadn't then Melody would wrap her arms around his waist in an attempt to keep him calm.

Finally, the emergency room door flew open, and Johanna recognized Nick from the library back in the spring. A tear slipped down his cheek, but it was the smile that overwhelmed his face. "We have a girl. Three pounds, five ounces. They expect her to be all right. And Addy is more wonderful than the day I married her."

Cheers rang through the waiting room. Drew raced to Nick and grabbed him in a bear hug. "Can I go back there?"

Nick shook his head. "Not yet. I'll let you know."

He appeared somewhat dejected, but he was still smiling. Drew hugged his wife. "We have a niece."

Mike wrapped his arm around Johanna's waist. She looked up at his face. His mouth was so close to hers. Only a whisper away. She only needed to tilt her head just a bit, and she could kiss him. She wanted to. Desperately, she wanted to.

A push came from behind Mike, deflecting the moment. Wyatt grinned at them. "Let's go get something to eat. We've been here for hours, and I'm starving."

fourteen

Nervous butterflies swarmed in Mike's gut for what seemed the millionth time since he'd awakened that morning. As he followed Johanna in the diner, he admitted the day had not gone as he had planned. Not at all.

He hadn't seen Lacy in quite some time, and it had been over three months since their failed date. He hoped she wouldn't still be angry with him. Or possibly that she wasn't working at dinnertime on a Saturday night.

He spied a dark-haired woman with her back to them. She didn't have to turn around. He knew it was Lacy.

"I've never been here before," Johanna said as she slid into the booth.

Wyatt moved into the inside of the booth on their side, while Gracie placed the baby's car seat in some wooden contraption designed to hold the whole thing.

"It's one of our favorite places to eat," Wyatt said. "Mike always orders meat loaf and mashed potatoes."

Mike scowled at his friend, and Wyatt laughed.

Gracie settled in beside Wyatt. She pointed to the menu. "Johanna, I always get the fried chicken. It's delicious."

The waitress walked up to their booth, and Mike blew out an audible sigh of relief when he saw the long red-haired woman whose name tag read SARAH. He'd be happy to take a "scraggly red hair" in his food today.

Johanna looked at him, her expression piqued with concern. "You okay?"

He wiped his hand across his face. "Just tired."

Sarah took their drink orders, but Johanna wanted to look at the menu a little longer before placing her order. Mike surveyed the room again. He hadn't seen Lacy since they'd first walked in. Maybe he'd been wrong, and the woman he'd seen wasn't her.

"What's the matter, Mike?"

Mike looked across the booth at his friend. Wyatt smirked, and Mike squinted at him. "Nothing's the matter, Wyatt."

Johanna looked up from the menu. "I think I'm going to try the chicken and dumplings."

Mike nodded. "Good choice."

Wyatt scoffed. "How would you know?"

Mike leaned toward Johanna. "He's right. I don't. But it sounds like a good choice."

Gracie and Johanna laughed, and Mike smirked at Wyatt.

Sarah came back with their soft drinks and took their orders. Greta started to fuss, and Gracie took her out of the car seat. Short blond hair stuck out all over the baby's head as if she'd stuck her finger in a light socket. She cooed and smiled at Gracie. The kid obviously wanted attention.

Mike noticed Johanna looked longingly at the little tyke. He had no doubt she would want a passel of kids. He hadn't had all that much experience with children, but he'd be willing to have as many as Johanna wanted, especially if they looked like her.

Gracie nodded to Johanna. "Would you like to hold her?"

Johanna perked up beside him. "You don't mind?"

"Of course not."

Wyatt moved the glasses out of the way while Gracie passed the baby over the table to Johanna. Mike watched as she nestled the girl close to her chest. Greta reached for her hair and cooed. Johanna traced her finger along the baby's cheek. "I'm so thankful Nick and Addy's baby is all right."

"Yes," they all agreed.

Mike couldn't take his eyes off Johanna with the baby. Everywhere he'd seen her with children she had taken to them naturally. And they'd always taken to her.

"Here's your food." Sarah stood beside them with a tray filled with their orders.

Mike inadvertently checked his food for any red hairs. He shook his head when he realized what he was doing. He'd have never done that if Lacy hadn't said what she had to him.

Once everyone received their plates, Wyatt said grace over their food. Johanna continued to hold Greta while she ate. He was impressed with how easy it seemed to be for her.

A shadow fell over him. He looked up and smiled, expecting to see Sarah returning to fill their glasses. It was Lacy.

"Hello, Wyatt. Mike." The dark-haired woman looked from one to the other. Disdain etched her features, and he knew this would not be a good visit. "I haven't seen you boys around here lately. You used to come in all the time."

Mike stiffened. His tongue stuck to the roof of his mouth. He'd done nothing wrong with Lacy. Nothing at all. But he had no idea what she would say or do.

Wyatt smiled up at her. "We've been busy." He pointed across the table to Johanna. Mike almost swallowed his tongue. What would Wyatt say to Lacy about Johanna? "As you can see, Gracie and I just had our second baby."

"I see that." Lacy smacked her chewing gum. "She's right pretty." She nudged Mike with her wrist. "How you doing?"

Mike forced his tongue to untwist. "Doing good."

This time she pointed to Johanna. "Who's your lady friend?"

Johanna's sweet, genuine, innocent, unknowing smile bowed her lips. "I'm Johanna Smith. It's nice to meet you."

Lacy nodded to her plate of food. "At least he bought you some dinner."

Johanna frowned and stiffened beside him. "What?"

She sneered at Mike. "You are paying for it, aren't you?"

Anger boiled within him. He knew she'd say something he didn't appreciate, but he hadn't imagined she'd say something that suggested he would be unkind to his date. He swallowed to keep from saying something he'd regret later. "Yes, I am. Thank you."

Lacy rolled her eyes and walked away.

"What was she talking about?" Johanna studied him. The confused expression that wrapped her face dug at his heart. He would explain everything to her on the way home.

Before he could respond, his cell phone rang. He pulled it out of his front pocket and read Nick's name on the screen. He pushed TALK. "Hey, Nick. Everything all right?"

He felt Wyatt, Gracie, and Johanna staring at him for any sign of trouble.

Nick still sounded elated. "Everything's great. I need you to do me a favor."

"Sure. Anything."

"Addy's water broke when she was making me rearrange the living room furniture. I've got just about all the furniture in the middle of the room."

"Okay."

"I wondered if you and Wyatt would go over there and put everything back for me. I can't get Drew to leave."

Drew's voice sounded in the distance. "Ain't no way I'm leaving my sister and my niece to go move furniture."

Mike laughed. "It's not a problem."

"Come on over to the hospital. I'll give you the keys to the house."

"Okay. See you after a while."

Mike hung up the phone and lifted his hands before the three of them attacked him at once for information. "Everything is fine. Nick just needs Wyatt and me to move some furniture at their house."

A collective sigh sounded around the booth.

"I'll take Johanna home then come back and get the keys and—"

Johanna frowned. "Mike, that's crazy. You don't need to drive to Hickory Hill then back. I'll just wait to go home until you're finished."

Mike shook his head. "It might be late, and I know your dad starts his early service at eight o'clock—"

Johanna cocked her head to the side. "I believe I've stayed up late before. I'll be fine."

Gracie interrupted their conversation. "Why don't you let me take her home?"

At the same time, Mike and Johanna said, "No."

"You don't need to do that," Johanna added.

Gracie put her napkin down in the middle of her plate. "I insist." She stood up and straightened her shirt. "Boys, you go pay for this, and I'll take Johanna home."

Johanna tried to decline again, but Gracie insisted.

Mike inwardly growled. Stubborn as a mule, Gracie would

never back down until she got her way. But he needed to talk to Johanna. He needed to explain about Lacy. He peered into her eyes, noting the hurt that filled them. "I want to take you home," he whispered.

She averted her gaze. "It's okay. Thank you for dinner."

﹡

"Tell me your address. I'll put it in my GPS so you don't have to keep telling me where to turn."

Johanna told Gracie her address then buckled her seat belt.

Gracie winked at her. "Greta loves to ride in the car. Maybe she'll get good and tired and sleep well for me when I get home."

Johanna forced herself to smile. She didn't understand what had happened at the diner, but right now, she simply wanted to go home and cry out to God.

"I love to drive through the country. It's so pretty." Gracie pointed out the windshield. "Look at those stars. Amazing."

Johanna nodded. Her mind kept replaying what the waitress had said. Obviously, Mike had dated the woman at some point, but it didn't make any sense to her that he would refuse to buy her dinner or pay for it or whatever she was talking about.

"I think I need to tell you about Lacy."

Johanna peered across the car at the woman she'd met only a few hours ago. "The waitress?"

"Yes. But I probably need to start at the beginning."

Johanna listened as Gracie told her about a no-women bet the four men had made several years ago, and how one by one they had all lost. She placed her finger on the side of her mouth. "Hmm. Except Mike. He's the winner. I guess that means you two get your wedding paid for."

"Oh, but, we're not—"

"Engaged?" Gracie raised her eyebrows and looked at her. "Honey, if Mike has anything to do with it, you will be."

Warmth traipsed up her neck at Gracie's words. She wanted him to ask her so badly. At least she thought she did. For a moment, earlier in the day, she'd thought he would ask her. But now, with what happened at the diner. . . She needed to know the whole story about the waitress. Surely, Mike was who she thought he was. He couldn't possibly have been fooling her family all this time.

Gracie popped her gum, and Johanna turned her attention back to the woman. Despite not knowing the woman very long, Johanna felt a natural drawing to her. Gracie seemed to be quite spirited, a real crackerjack, as her mother would say. But, she also seemed as genuine as she was spirited.

She lifted her right hand off the wheel. "Now, let me tell you about Lacy. Mike had this crush on the girl forever. It was ridiculous. The man didn't know anything about her, but he had a crush on her just the same." Gracie reached over and patted Johanna's leg. "I know that probably hurts your feelings a bit, but I promise you the man is over the moon about you."

Johanna peered out the windshield. It did sting that Mike once had a crush on another woman. She remembered all the times she'd felt she should have experienced some sort of jealousy for Gavin, but she hadn't. She felt it now for Mike. The thought of Mike holding another woman's hand or looking at another woman the way he looked at her—it just made her sick to her stomach.

Gracie sneaked a quick peek back at the baby, who'd fallen asleep, then turned around and focused on the road. "So three years later Mike finally gets up the nerve to ask Lacy on a dinner date. They go, but he brings her back early, evidently without buying her dinner. It didn't work out."

Johanna frowned. "What happened?"

Gracie shrugged. "We don't really know. Mike won't say." Gracie turned down the air in the car. "Would you mind to turn around and fix Greta's head? It's kind of leaning over crooked."

Johanna turned around and folded a section of Greta's soft pink blanket. Gently, lifting the child's head, she tucked the blanket against the side of the car seat. Greta let out a contented sigh, and Johanna's heart melted. She turned back around. "Greta is absolutely precious."

"Especially when she's asleep." Gracie chuckled and swatted the air. "I'm just kidding. Thanks. But, back to Mike. You've known Mike a few months now. Have you ever heard him talk bad about anyone?"

Johanna thought a moment. "No, I haven't."

"That's just it. He won't talk about it. Just says they disagreed about faith. But he won't even tell us what he means by that." The GPS announced their arrival to her house, and Gracie pulled into the driveway. "Looks like we're here."

Johanna opened the door. "Thanks for bringing me home. It was really good to meet you." She paused. "And thanks for explaining things to me."

Gracie grabbed her hand before she got out. "Listen. Mike is a good man, and he is absolutely crazy about you. The fact that Mike McCauley won't talk about what happened during that date with Lacy speaks volumes about her, not him. Do you understand?"

Johanna smiled and nodded. "Yes. Thanks."

Once she stepped out of the car, the weight of the day bore down on her. Exhausted, she dragged her feet up the porch steps and into the house.

Her father met her at the door. "Are the baby and the mother okay?"

Johanna smacked her forehead with her hand. How could she have forgotten to call and update her family? "Daddy, I'm sorry I didn't call. Yes. The baby girl and her mother are fine. She'll be in NICU for a while, so we'll need to keep praying for her, but she's doing well."

"What's her name?" her mother asked.

"They haven't named her yet, but I think I'll go back to the hospital after church tomorrow and visit with Addy."

Her mother wrapped her arm around Johanna. "That sounds like a great idea, but you look exhausted. Go upstairs, get a warm bath, and then get in bed."

"Mama, that sounds like a wonderful plan."

Johanna made her way up the stairs. After starting her bath, she slipped into the warm waters and rested her head against the cool porcelain.

The waitress had surprised her. Her words had stung worse than any wasp sting she'd ever received. The fact that Mike once had a crush on another woman and for such a long time stabbed at her heart. Three years. She'd only known him three months.

God, Gracie says he is head over heels for me. But was he the same for the waitress? How can I know that what he feels for me, that what I feel for him is real? That it's from You?

God seemed especially quiet. Or maybe she was just tired and therefore not listening very well. She got out of the bath and slipped into her nightgown. Crawling into bed, she closed her eyes. She'd have to wait until tomorrow to figure it out.

fifteen

After taking one last long drink of her coffee, Johanna scooped up the present she'd bought for Nick and Addy's baby from the passenger's seat then walked into the hospital. She hadn't slept a moment the night before. Though she'd prayed God would allow her mind to rest, she continued to replay the concern and tension in the waiting room while Addy gave birth. Then her heart would swell anew with thanksgiving when Nick burst through the door with good news. Then Lacy's contemptuous expression and tone would push to the forefront of her mind, and she'd try to remember and believe all Gracie had said on the drive home.

But her mind was a tricky thing. It kept conjuring up images of Mike with Lacy on a date. She envisioned the woman's long brown hair cascading down one shoulder. Beyond the glasses, her sultry green eyes sparkled beneath long eyelashes. Looks of longing and adoration shone from Mike's gaze, and for a moment, his tongue dropped from his mouth like a dog that panted for water.

Get a grip, Johanna. Shaking her head, she blew out a breath at the dramatics of her thoughts. She pushed the elevator button. *Took that image a bit far, I think. Believe I'm feeling some good old-fashioned, green-eyed jealousy now.*

Though she'd wrestled with the fact that Mike had liked another woman, God reminded her over and again through the night that Mike had proven himself to be a man of God.

She was reminded of Gracie's words of him not being willing to speak poorly of Lacy. Of Mike's prayer for Nick and Addy and their baby at the hospital. . . The way Johanna had seen Mike help his mother and his father at their house. The fact that he'd helped his friends at a moment's call. Even before Johanna knew it was Mike, the articles he'd written the past several years spoke of a love for God that could only come from Him.

She knew Mike to be a good man. A godly man. And she loved him.

The elevator door opened and Johanna stepped onto the maternity floor. Her favorite part of the hospital—she smiled at the teddy bears, lambs, sunshine, and balloon murals on the walls. After asking one of the nurses about Addy's location, she walked down the hall to the room.

Several voices pealed out from within the room. A wave of shyness washed over Johanna, and she gripped the present tighter. Yesterday, she'd experienced such a deep concern for the woman she'd met only one other time, that she simply had to see her again, to tell her how happy she was the baby had delivered safely.

Fearing Mike would be inside the room, and yet wanting him to be inside the room, Johanna willed her feet to move forward. Gingerly, she knocked on the doorjamb.

"Come on in," a voice boomed from inside. If she remembered correctly, it sounded like Drew.

Hesitantly, Johanna slipped inside the door. Seeing Addy in the bed, she ducked her chin and waved. "Hi. You may not remember me—"

Addy motioned her inside. "Of course, I remember you, Johanna. Please come on in."

Though her face was pale and her hair pulled back in a knot

that stuck out at odd angles, Addy glowed like a woman who'd just been handed the whole world. Heat warmed Johanna's cheeks when she looked around the crowded room at Drew, Melody and Nick, and two women she'd never met before.

Addy motioned to her guests. "You know Nick, Drew, and Melody."

They nodded, and Johanna smiled back at them.

She pointed to the woman with short sandy-blond hair. "This is my mother, Amanda." Then she pointed to the dark-haired woman. "And Nick's mother, Renee."

"It's nice to meet both of you."

Renee grabbed Johanna's hand. "Honey, we've just been dying to meet Mike's girl."

"Mom!" Nick groaned.

Amanda added, "She's every bit as pretty as Mike said."

"Mother!" Addy and Drew said at the same time.

Feeling dizzy from too much coffee and not enough food, Johanna prayed her knees would stay strong. She swallowed the embarrassment that welled in her throat then remembered the present crumbling beneath her death grip. She handed it to Addy. "I got the baby a present."

"You didn't have to do that."

"I wanted to."

Amanda patted Johanna's shoulder. "Renee and I are going to go check on our husbands. They went to get food over an hour ago."

Renee chuckled. "After driving straight through from Florida last night, we're starving."

Melody nudged Drew's arm. "Come on. We'll go, too. I'm hungry myself."

Drew frowned. "I'm fine."

Nick punched his arm. "Your sister is fine. I'm right here for her. She is my wife, you know." He turned to Johanna. "We can't get the guy to leave."

Melody grabbed his hand and pulled to try to get him up. "Let's let them be alone for a little while. We don't have to leave the hospital."

Reluctantly, Drew stood and followed his wife out of the room, leaving Nick, Addy, and Johanna alone. She took a step toward the door. "I'll let you two have some time alone."

"No, please." Addy motioned to the chair Drew had been sitting in. "Sit down. I'd like to visit a minute." She lifted up the package. "Besides, I'm dying to see what you brought."

Johanna wrung her hands together and sat down. This couple had occupied much of her thoughts and prayers in the last twenty-four hours, but actually sitting with them, she realized she really didn't know them at all.

Addy unwrapped the present and pulled out the pink-and-white sleeper outfit Johanna found at the department store. "Thank you so much." She laid the gift back in the box and handed it to Nick. "I remember you quite well from the library event."

Johanna nodded. "It was a good event. Having the two of you there made it a huge success. The children enjoyed the calf and the seed planting. I'm sure it was a first experience at petting a calf and planting a seed for many of them."

Nick lifted his right foot and rested it on his left knee. "I think you had them going reading that book as well. They watched you like they were watching a TV show."

Johanna grinned. Despite her normal bashfulness, when she read for children, something in her seemed to click, and her voice inflected with the events of the story.

"This may sound odd for me to say since this is only the second time we've met." Addy shifted in the bed. "But you're a godsend for Mike."

Johanna bit the inside of her lip. She already felt woozy from having not eaten breakfast. She didn't know how much more embarrassment she could take before she plastered the floor with her body.

"If that ain't the truth," Nick added. "I've never seen the man so happy. And he's the one who wanted a wife first."

"Nick!" Addy exclaimed.

Trying to change the subject, Johanna asked, "How's the baby?"

Nick smiled. "Perfect."

"Wonderful," Addy added.

"Have you picked out a name for her?"

Addy leaned forward. "Don't tell, but we're going with the name I picked out when I was fifteen."

Johanna furrowed her brows.

Nick huffed. "Yeah, the woman hounded me to marry her since she was no bigger than knee high to a grasshopper."

"Hey now." Addy's eyebrows rose and she glared at him.

He lifted his hands in surrender. "Okay. Okay. There's a little more to it than that."

Johanna chuckled at their antics. "So what is her name?"

Addy folded her hands in her lap. "Amanda Renee. After our mothers."

"When can you see her again?"

Addy peered at the door. Johanna turned and saw that a nurse had walked into the room.

"Looks like Nick and I can go right now." Slowly, Addy started to get up from the bed. Nick grabbed her hand to help her.

Johanna jumped out of her chair and headed for the door. "It was so good to talk with you both. I'm glad the baby is well."

Now standing, Addy shuffled around the bed. "She'll be in NICU for a little while, but she's doing well. Thanks for coming."

After saying their good-byes, Johanna walked out of the hospital and to her car. With her stomach queasy, she decided to head home. Her mind could think about Mike all it wanted, but her body needed some food.

❧

Mike had been waiting at the pond for well over two hours. He'd gone to the early service at Johanna's church, but Pastor Smith told him she'd felt so burdened for Nick and Addy that she'd visited them in the hospital instead.

Knowing Mike was anxious to talk to Johanna, the older man suggested he head to their house and wait for her there. Mike stood and paced in front of the bench. He looked at his watch. *Surely, she'll be here soon. I wanted to talk with her before everyone got back from church.*

He picked up the single red rose he'd bought for her, signifying she was his one love. He gazed up at the clear sky. *God, I pray she'll accept me.*

"Mike, what are you doing up here?"

He turned and saw Johanna making her way up the hill to the pond. Beautiful in a light-green shirt that tied around the waist and white pants, she'd pulled back the sides of her hair in a clip of some kind. The breeze caught several wisps and blew them around her jaw. He spread his arms wide, still holding the rose in his hand. "I'm waiting for you."

She finished her trek then pulled away a strand of hair that stuck to her lip. "I saw your truck in the driveway, and—" She looked at the rose, and the color of her cheeks deepened. "Why are you waiting for me?"

"I need to talk to you." Mike stepped close to her. She peered up at him, and the expression of love shining from her eyes both humbled him and gave him courage. He caressed her cheek with the back of his hand. "I love you, Johanna."

"I know." She reached up and cupped her hand against his jaw. "I love you, too."

He couldn't resist. He lowered his head and gently touched his lips to hers. Releasing her, he started to lift his head but she pulled him back to her, kissing him fully with passion and love. Unable to breathe and feeling too much emotion at one time, Mike stepped back. "Johanna, let me explain about Lacy."

She took a step closer to him. "I already know."

He stepped back. "Then I need to tell you about the bet."

She inched closer to him again. "Already know about that, too."

He cocked his head. "What else do you know?"

She pointed to his pocket. "I know there's a ring in that front pocket for me." She lifted her face and kissed his lips. "Am I right?"

His jaw dropped. "Johanna Smith!" He laid the back of his hand on her forehead. "Are you sick?"

She stomped her foot like a child. "Actually, I am a little queasy. I drank two cups of coffee and haven't had anything to eat yet because I was up all night thinking about Nick and Addy and their baby." She peered at him and stuck out her bottom lip. "And about you."

Mike let out a loud whoop. "Johanna, you are a hoot."

She wrinkled her nose at him as she pointed beneath her

eyes. "Do these bags look funny to you?"

"I love the bags under your eyes." He touched her cheek. "And the dimple in your cheek. And your beautiful eyes." He placed a quick kiss on her mouth. "And your perfect lips." He raised one eyebrow as he stared at her. "So, you think I have something in my pocket?"

A full smile spread across her lips as she nodded. He reached into his pocket and pulled out the box. Opening it, she gasped at the small, delicate ring he'd picked out for her. She whispered, "It's beautiful."

Mike knelt down. He spread one hand toward the pond. "I wanted to ask you in your spot." He took her hand in his and peered into her eyes. "Johanna Smith, I love you. Will you be my wife?"

She nodded and he jumped up, pulled her into his arms, and swung her around. Placing her back on her feet, he kissed her again. Releasing her, he searched her face. "How did you know?"

She brushed a strand of hair off her cheek. "You and Daddy were pretty obvious yesterday."

Mike laughed. "I thought we were being pretty sneaky."

Disbelief washed over Johanna's face.

He wrapped his arms around her. "I'm glad you bumped into me last spring."

She lifted up three fingers. "Took three times to get your attention."

"It will never take that long again."

sixteen

Johanna could hardly believe nine months had passed, and tomorrow she would be Mike's wife. True to their promise, Wyatt, Nick, and Drew had all been intricately involved in the planning of the ceremony, and they took care of all the bills. At first, her father had adamantly declined their offer, until they suggested he donate the money he'd have spent on the wedding to a couple at the church who felt called to foreign missions. Her father said he couldn't turn down an offer like that.

Her father had insisted he help Mike's parents pay and prepare the food for the rehearsal dinner. Johanna looked at the grandfather clock in the living room. The rehearsal had gone splendidly earlier in the day. Any minute Mike and his friends would arrive for dinner.

"Do I look okay?"

Johanna turned toward her now thirteen-year-old sister, Bethany, who was blossoming into a young woman. She wore a light-blue shorts outfit with her long blond hair rolled in soft curls. She smiled, exposing the aqua bands put on her metal braces to match her bridesmaid dress. "You look lovely."

Amber flitted through the room. She held one silver sandal in the air. "I can't find my other shoe. Have you seen it?"

Johanna shook her head.

Bethany grabbed her hand and led her toward the door. "I think I saw it outside."

"Outside? Why would it be outside?"

Bethany shrugged. "You know Max likes your shiny shoes."

With a squeal, Amber rushed outside.

Johanna bit back a laugh. Pride swelled within her for her sister. Amber graduated from high school earning a full music scholarship to a nearby small college. She'd even gotten an A in math.

The back door opened, and Johanna checked to see if it was Mike. Gavin peeked around the corner instead. "Hey."

She waved at her longtime friend. "Hi."

"Ready for tomorrow?"

"Definitely."

Amber walked in with two shiny silver shoes on her feet. She wrapped her arms around Gavin in a big hug. The silly grin that spread across his face made Johanna chuckle. His father continued to do well with the new medicine he'd started taking several months before. Amber already planned to spend much of her summer helping Gavin's mother care for her brood. Johanna knew Gavin wouldn't mind seeing Amber more often.

She made her way past them and looked out the kitchen window at her mom and dad grilling steaks, potatoes, and corn on the cob. It hadn't taken a lot of convincing when Johanna told Mike and their parents she simply wanted a cookout at her house for their wedding rehearsal dinner. Her mom and Mike's mom both had the reputation of being some of the best cooks in this part of the state.

Mike's truck pulled into the driveway, followed by his parents' car. Johanna ran outside to greet them.

"Where's your mother?" His mom lifted a pie from the backseat.

"My parents are around back, grilling."

She nodded for his dad to get the other dishes out of the backseat. "Come on. We need to help them get everything finished."

His dad winked and kissed Johanna's forehead then looked at his wife. "Whatever you say, dear."

As they walked away, Johanna smiled up at her fiancé. His sandy-brown locks were newly cut, and she reached up and touched the shorter hair. He growled as he kissed her lips. "One more day."

Another car sounded in the driveway, interrupting the moment. Johanna waved as Gracie and Wyatt pulled up in their minivan. She made her way to them and unbuckled two-and-a-half-year-old little Wyatt, while Gracie lifted out the barely toddling Greta.

Bethany ran up to Gracie. "You want me to take them to the backyard?"

Gracie sighed. "That would be wonderful."

Johanna watched as little Wyatt raced to the swing set her parents hadn't gotten rid of since she and her sisters were little. Greta was determined to walk, so Bethany had to hold her hand and move slowly behind the rambunctious Wyatt Jr.

Before Johanna could invite them inside, Drew and Melody pulled up in their Jeep. Nick, Addy, and their baby Amanda piled out of the backseat. Johanna reached for the baby and clapped. "Come here, big girl."

The sweet cherub cackled and launched out of her mother's arms toward Johanna. Even though she was still a bit on the smaller side, Amanda continued to thrive and develop as she should.

The group meandered to the backyard and sat in lawn chairs

beneath a large oak tree.

"Should be ready in about fifteen minutes," her mother called from beside the grill.

"Do you need any help?" Melody said.

Mike's mother responded, "Nope. We're fine."

Johanna's heart warmed as she watched Mike's parents and her parents work together on the food. Mike's mother had come such a long way in the last several months. They'd even been attending her dad's church. Johanna knew God was healing her heart. Mike had given full credit to God for that. He insisted it was no coincidence that as his mother's love for Johanna blossomed, she remembered God's Word contained a promise—a promise of hope for the future. While it embarrassed Johanna whenever Mike praised God for bringing her into his mother's life, she was deeply grateful for the bond that had grown between her and the woman who would soon be her mother-in-law.

Johanna smiled at Mike and his friends. They sat in a line of sorts beside each other. By the expressions on their faces she could see they were about to give each other a hard time about something.

Addy asked, "Are you all ready for tomorrow, Johanna?"

Johanna nodded. "I am. Hair at nine. Makeup at ten. Manicures and pedicures at eleven. A quick lunch then the wedding at two. I'm not going to have time to be nervous tomorrow."

"Have you seen the cake your mom made yet?" asked Melody. "It can't be any more beautiful than the one she made for Drew and me."

Johanna shook her head. "She's keeping it in the refrigerator in the garage. She won't let me see it."

Nick smacked at Mike's leg. "Are you ready for tomorrow, buddy?"

"Oh, yes." Mike grinned then wiggled his eyebrows at Johanna. She felt her cheeks flush.

"Really?" Nick crossed his arms in front of his chest. "You're ready for a woman to holler at you every morning for leaving stubbles in the sink when you shave?"

Addy squealed, "Nick Martin!"

Drew chimed in, "Or to grouch at you because you've forgotten to pick your socks up off the floor."

Melody cocked her head to one side. "Do you want me to show them right now that I can take you down?"

Wyatt howled. "And the two a.m. cravings for ice cream when she's seven months pregnant are killer."

Gracie smirked. "I know. And we're going to do it again."

The whole group gasped and looked from Gracie to Wyatt. Johanna sputtered, "Are you pregnant again?"

Gracie wrinkled her nose and pointed her thumb at Wyatt. "It's his fault."

A mischievous grin spread across Wyatt's lips. "I'll take credit for it."

They laughed, and her father called that the food was ready. After enjoying a delicious meal and nice fellowship, the crew loaded up and headed home. Johanna and Mike walked up to the pond and sat on the bench in silence as the sun set over the still waters.

Johanna rested her temple on Mike's shoulder. "This time tomorrow night we'll be husband and wife."

Mike wrapped his arm around her and pulled her closer to him. "I can hardly wait."

"I'm awestruck at God's blessing."

"As am I."

Johanna turned her face and kissed his jaw. "I love you, Mike."

Mike cleared his throat and stood. "I think we'd best be getting back to the house."

She stuck out her bottom lip. "What's wrong?"

He bent down and kissed her bottom lip then quickly stepped away from her. "You're entirely too cute, smell entirely too good, and I love you entirely too much. And you're not my wife until tomorrow."

Understanding filled her mind, and Johanna laughed. She stood up and grabbed his hand in hers. "Then let's head back to the house." As they walked down the hill, she leaned closer to him and whispered, "I can't wait for tomorrow, either."

epilogue

Two years later

Mike had never known his wife's true strength until she gripped his collar with her fist. "You've got to get me to the hospital right now."

"I know. I'm trying." Mike moved frantically through the house in search of the truck keys. He always put them on the key rack in the kitchen. Johanna had been the last one to drive the truck, and she never put them in the same place twice. *There is no way I'm going to mention that now.*

Out of sheer desperation, he opened the refrigerator. There they were, sitting on the butter. He shook his head. *I'm not even going to try to think about what weird concoction she was probably eating.* He yelled, "I got them."

"It's about time." She heaved from the other room. "I think I'm going to have this baby on the floor."

The last few months of Johanna's pregnancy had proved extremely interesting. Mike would argue with anyone that he had the sweetest, kindest wife in the world. She loved being his wife. She'd longed for children, and God blessed their prayers with this pregnancy. But he had no idea what happened to the woman he married when she reached her seventh month. His father promised him she would return to her senses soon.

He walked back into the living room and found Johanna gripping the back of a chair. She was leaned forward with her hand on the bottom of her stomach. "This is the worst pain in the world. It's like someone is stabbing me with a knife." She lifted up her face and gritted her teeth. "Feel this."

Mike touched her belly. It was hard as a basketball that had been inflated too much and was about to pop. And his wife, and he loved her with all his heart, she looked like she was about to pop.

When her breathing slowed and she took several long exhales, he wrapped his arm around her and hustled her out to the truck. He ran back in the house to get her purse and the baby bag. By the time he returned, she was gripping the door handle and groaning. Another contraction. He looked at his watch. It couldn't have been more than two minutes. They were coming fast.

Praying that God would give him grace for no red lights and no tractors or slow drivers in front of him, Mike pulled out of the driveway. He had turned onto the main road that led straight to the hospital when Johanna grabbed the door handle as well as his arm. He peeked at his wife. An expression of pure agony wrenched her face, and Mike begged God to ease the pain, even if just a little. Or at least to give her the strength to hang in there.

Two more contractions hit by the time he'd made the additional five-minute drive. Once there, he helped her out of the truck. She moved slow, and Mike wished he'd thought to get a wheelchair before he'd tried to get her out of the truck. Another contraction hit before they made it inside. He held her tight as she bent over and winced. Once inside, he blew out a slow breath. *Thank You, God, that we've made it to the hospital.*

He walked to the nurse at the front desk. He tried to remain calm, but he was slowly losing all capacity to do so each time he saw the extreme agony on Johanna's face. "My wife needs drugs. She's in a lot of pain, and I can't take it anymore." The woman harrumphed at him as she shoved a piece of paper across the desk.

Okay, that had not exactly come out in the best of ways. *God, I can't take it, though. She's dying, and I can't do anything to help her. It's even my fault, Lord. It's my fault.*

Another contraction kicked in, and Johanna doubled over again. Believing Johanna, the woman ran around the desk, grabbed a wheelchair from another room, and sat her in it. The nurse looked at him. "I've got to let the doctor know she's here. Hang tight for just a minute."

She started to walk away, but then she turned back and looked at him. "Are you okay? You look like you're about to be sick."

He motioned for her to go on. "I'm fine." He swallowed the knot in his throat and pulled at the collar of his T-shirt. He'd be fine as soon as someone did something to help Johanna's pain.

The emergency door opened behind them and a familiar voice said, "Nurse! I need help. Nurse! Right now!"

Mike turned to see Drew helping a very full-term Melody through the door.

"Hurry!" He yelled again. Mike saw the look of panic in his friend's eyes. "Her water broke. Like ten minutes ago."

Melody muttered, "It's okay, Drew." She blew out a breath. "It's supposed to." She blew out another one. "It's going to be fine."

Drew's jaw dropped when he saw Mike. "What are you doing here?"

Mike pointed to his wife with his free hand. She held tight to his other, which was fine with him if it stopped some of her pain. "Johanna's in labor."

Drew pointed to Melody. "She is, too." He grabbed Mike's sleeve. "Man, this is awful. I can't take it. I can't do anything to help her."

Melody grabbed at Drew's hand. "Would you chill out?" She groaned, as a contraction must have hit her.

Johanna's grip on his hand tightened, as a contraction must have hit her as well. If the contraction didn't hurry up and subside, she was going to break every bone in his hand. Once again, he'd have never dreamed his sweet, angelic Johanna to be so strong.

The doors opened again and Wyatt pushed in Gracie in a wheelchair. She smiled at Mike and Drew. "Time for baby number four." She grimaced for a moment with her hand on top of her belly then let out a slow breath. "Whew. That was a good one."

Mike wiped his brow with his free hand when Johanna finally loosened her tight grip. "You have got to be kidding me. If Addy goes into labor—"

"Already here," Melody muttered. "Called an hour ago."

Looking frantic, Drew leaned down and grabbed Melody's hand. "Don't talk, honey. Just concentrate on you and the baby. Everything is going to be fine."

Melody glared at him. "I am fine. You're the one freaking out."

"Oops." Johanna squeaked. "My water just broke."

Mike looked down at the liquid that ran down the front of the wheelchair. Tears rolled down Johanna's cheeks, and Mike couldn't decipher if she was scared, excited, happy, or simply still in so much pain it was leaking from her eyes. He motioned for the woman who'd gotten them a wheelchair. "Nurse! We've got to go."

The nurse shook her head and smiled. "It's baby night." She motioned for two other people to take Melody and Gracie, while she wheeled Johanna to the delivery room. "We've got us a full house."

As gingerly as possible, he helped Johanna out of the wheelchair. The nurse produced a gown of sorts. "Let's get her out of those clothes and into something more comfortable."

The woman worked with an efficiency Mike couldn't help but admire as she undressed and redressed his wife. He got the socks from the bag and did put those on for her, but it took him almost as long to do that as it took the nurse to change Johanna's clothes.

Johanna was calm as the nurse inserted her IV, checked her pulse, and felt her stomach. The woman looked at Mike. "Her contractions seem to be coming about every two minutes." She looked at Johanna. "I'm going to check to see where we are."

Again, Mike took Johanna's hand in his. She gripped it with the strength of a man, but Mike's heart melted when she looked up at him and tears streamed down her cheeks. "I'm scared," she whispered.

With his free hand, he brushed her hair away from her face. "You're doing so good, Johanna. I'm so proud of you."

She nodded, seemingly revived by his words. *Dear God, please let her be okay. Please let our baby come safely. Let the child be healthy. Keep me strong, too, Lord.*

The nurse pulled the curtain and checked Johanna. "Ten centimeters. She's ready." She turned to a woman standing in the doorway. "Go get the doctor in here." She patted the top of Johanna's leg. "Looks like you got here just in time, hon."

Things happened in a whirlwind after that with people coming and going and Johanna squeezing his hand as if she would never let go. He couldn't watch. He was too scared, too excited, too preoccupied with whispering words of encouragement in Johanna's ear.

A cry sounded through the room as the doctor lifted up the baby. His baby. Their baby. "It's a boy."

Tears swelled in his eyes, and he placed his forehead against Johanna's. "Good job, Johanna. You did so good."

The nurse wiped the baby off and placed him on Johanna's chest for just a moment. Mike kissed his wife. "I love you, Johanna." He kissed his son. "And I love you."

Mike cut the cord then he picked up his son and walked him to the table where they would check to make sure he was fine.

After kissing Johanna once more, he walked to the waiting room to tell their family the news. With a happiness and joy he'd never known in all his life, he pushed open the doors and announced, "A baby boy. Seven pounds even."

His parents and hers squealed and ran up to hug him. "And he's beautiful."

"How's Johanna?" her father asked.

"She's perfect. She's wonderful. She's absolutely amazing."

Johanna's mother giggled. "But she's okay after the delivery, right?"

Mike laughed and nodded. "Yes."

He looked around the room and saw Nick's parents and Drew and Addy's parents, and Wyatt's and Gracie's. "Have you heard anything from any of them yet?"

"Not yet," Wyatt's father said. He grabbed Mike's hand in a firm shake. "But congratulations." For the next few minutes, he hugged the people who had been such an integral part of his life. He'd grown up with these people's sons, and they'd been like second parents to him. They'd seen him through thick and thin—teen years, farming, the death of his brother—everything he'd ever gone through and lived through. He was suddenly overwhelmed with thanksgiving that they would all be here at the same time.

As Mike turned to walk back to his wife and new son, Nick burst through the doors. He yelled, "A boy. Nine pounds, fifteen ounces."

His and Addy's families squealed.

Before they had time to even hug him, the door opened again. Wyatt called, "A boy. Six pounds, three ounces."

Mike laughed. It seemed too absurd for words that they were all having babies on the same day, and all boys.

Drew pushed through the doors, whooping like a wild man. "It's a boy." He high-fived his dad and lifted his mom in the air and twirled her around. "But we got us a surprise! Remember how Melody refused any ultrasounds after reading an article about. . ." Drew swatted the air. "Oh, I can't remember what it was about. Anyway, there were two of them in there. Two boys. Five pounds, six ounces, and six pounds, one ounce." He shook his head. "I knew she looked awful big for just one kid."

The men shook hands and congratulated each other. Five boys born on the same day. Drew sucked in his breath and hooked his fingers through his jeans' belt loops. "Yep. It's pretty cool that we all had boys on the same day." He shrugged. "Course, I don't see none of y'all having two babies at one time."

Wyatt huffed. "Whatever. I have four kids. Double what you got."

"Well, mine was the biggest," Nick added, pointing to his chest.

Mike crossed his arms in front of his chest. "Mine was born first."

Drew puffed out his chest. "Oh yeah, well, I bet you my sons. . ."

A Letter To Our Readers

Dear Reader:

In order that we might better contribute to your reading enjoyment, we would appreciate your taking a few minutes to respond to the following questions. We welcome your comments and read each form and letter we receive. When completed, please return to the following:

Fiction Editor
Heartsong Presents
PO Box 719
Uhrichsville, Ohio 44683

1. Did you enjoy reading *Game of Love* by Jennifer Johnson?
   ❏ Very much! I would like to see more books by this author!
   ❏ Moderately. I would have enjoyed it more if

   _____

   _____

   _____

2. Are you a member of **Heartsong Presents**? ❏ Yes ❏ No
   If no, where did you purchase this book? _____

   _____

3. How would you rate, on a scale from 1 (poor) to 5 (superior), the cover design? _____

4. On a scale from 1 (poor) to 10 (superior), please rate the following elements.

   ____ Heroine   ____ Plot
   ____ Hero   ____ Inspirational theme
   ____ Setting   ____ Secondary characters

5. These characters were special because? _____

_____

_____

6. How has this book inspired your life? _____

_____

_____

7. What settings would you like to see covered in future
Heartsong Presents books? _____

_____

_____

8. What are some inspirational themes you would like to see
treated in future books? _____

_____

_____

9. Would you be interested in reading other **Heartsong
Presents** titles? ❏ Yes ❏ No

10. Please check your age range:
❏ Under 18   ❏ 18–24
❏ 25–34   ❏ 35–45
❏ 46–55   ❏ Over 55

Name _____

Occupation _____

Address _____

City, State, Zip_____

E-mail _____

DELAWARE WEDDINGS

3 stories in 1

Choices from the past put three modern Delaware women's hearts in limbo today. Can new romances in their lives open doors for forgiveness and love?

Contemporary, paperback, 352 pages, 5.1875" x 8 "

Hearts♥ng

Presents

Great Inspirational Romance
at a Great Price!

Heartsong Presents books are inspirational romances in contemporary and historical settings, designed to give you an enjoyable, spirit-lifting reading experience. You can choose wonderfully written titles from some of today's best authors like Wanda E. Brunstetter, Mary Connealy, Susan Page Davis, Cathy Marie Hake, Joyce Livingston, and many others.

When ordering quantities less than six, above titles are $3.99 each.
Not all titles may be available at time of order.